FAKE FLOWERS

graham lironi

fake flowers

© Graham Lironi 2021

ISBN 978-1-8384052-5-0

Published by Rymour Books
45 Needless Road
PERTH
PH2 0LE

http://www.rymour.co.uk

cover and book design by Ian Spring
printed by Imprint Digital, Exeter, Devon

A CIP record for this book
is available from the British Library

The paper used in this book is approved
by the Forest Stewardship Council

ACKNOWLEDGEMENTS

Thanks to Steven Morris for the back cover portrait of the artist as a young man snorkelling in L'Estartit, Ian Spring for the cover design and to everyone who has helped in the production of this volume

Graham Lironi 2021

FOR ALLISON
a life lived is surreal or nada

CONTENTS

foreword
i can stop time
(the persistence of memory)

afterword
my mum can stop time
(the disintegration of the persistence of memory)

postscript
a return to the dalí triangle

foreword

i can
stop time
(the persistence
of memory)

The morning after the night before, fresh from having consigned paternity test results into the dustbin for the second time, though *this* time before opening the envelope, I entered the newsroom to discover I'd gained a superpower: I could stop time.

In an instant, the reporters stopped reporting. The interviewers stopped interviewing. The subs stopped subbing. The gossips stopped gossiping. The schemers stopped scheming. The competitors stopped competing. The daydreamers stopped daydreaming.

Acutely aware of my entirely unintentional superpower, I feigned obliviousness to it and fought to remain fully focussed on maintaining my purposeful stride across the suddenly vast expanse of the open plan newsroom to my ultimate destination. The editor's office. I was a grown man reduced to putting one foot in front of the other with all the confidence of a new-born Bambi attempting to find her feet. Determined to resist an urge to turn and confront the prying eyes boring into my nape already blooming crimson, I knocked on the door.

'Come in,' came the usual world-weary command. Then, seeing it was me, 'Shut the door behind you and take a pew.'

Kerr scrutinised me. His fingers interlaced across the swollen belly straining the buttons of his Far Eastern slave trade produced shirt, twiddling his newspaper print-stained thumbs. Rocking back and forth on his rickety chair as though daring it to collapse under the stress, he weighed up how best to broach the matter at hand.

'You look like shit.'

'And *good morning* to you too.'

'Need some time out?'

'I need to fill it.'

'Good!' he said, slapping his desk before pausing, still uncertain how best to proceed. 'If you're *really* fine...'

'I am.'

' ...Then I want the full inside story; the unexpurgated, definitive first-hand account. Spare me no details. Don't worry about word count; I'm not looking for the usual op ed. We can serialise it if need be. I want the full bhuna. Take as long as you want. As long as I have it by Wednesday.'

'Here it is,' I said, extracting a wad of freshly printed pages from my battered satchel and dumping it on his desk. 'I couldn't sleep. Couldn't stop re-living last night. Already it exists only in my memory. Which is notoriously unreliable. So I had to write it all down before I forget. And to see if putting it down on paper might yield some kind of catharsis. I've called it *Fake Flowers*.'

'This looks more like a bloody book,' Kerr remarked, rifling through the pages as his phone rang at the exact moment my own mobile started beeping...

one

the dalí
triangle
summer

Submerged, plunged into the all-pervasive silence, save for my hypnotic rhythmic breathing resounding through the snorkel, mesmerised by a shape-shifting shoal of shimmering yellow and silver shimmying beneath, I swam from the shore, taking casual breaststrokes, hugging the rocks. A shaft of light penetrated deep below the surface to illuminate the Med's sandy bed. My mask misting, I reached out a magnified hand to touch a jagged rock to steady myself and gain a foothold. Resurfacing, I removed the mask to wipe it clean from condensation and stole a glance back to shore. Grace waved with abandon and I reciprocated self-consciously before replacing my mask, reinserting the snorkel and re-submerging. I tasted the sharp fresh tang of the salty sea, felt the rays of the sun burn my shoulders, took a deep breath, and revelled in the moment I'd been fantasising about for the last eleven months.

We'd sped straight from Girona airport in the hired pillar-box red Mini convertible, past fields of giant sunkissed sunflowers, impressionistic blurry heads bursting in cheerful orange and yellow bloom towering alongside, a riot of CinemaScope Technicolor stretching on tiptoes up to the sun that shone its full afternoon rays down on us. We were headed to L'Estartit, a destination suggested by Grace, drawn by a multitude of fading sun-dappled kaleidoscopic Kodachrome memories of family holidays spent cavorting on an infinite stretch of golden sand fringing a clear shallow aquamarine Med, tumbling topsy-turvy in the washing machine white horses galloping to shore.

It was while I ordered my first *cerveza* of the day at the beach bar that Grace, having lit a *Marlboro Red*, struck up an instant rapport with the barman and our holiday was destined to shift gear and accelerate into a whole other Dalí-shaped dimension.

It was the following day, after a further mesmerising underwater exploration, when Grace announced she required a refreshment and a break from her absorption in Lorca that, on revisiting the beach bar, we found ourselves sharing a table with the barman, who was finishing his lunch break tapas. Everything flowered from there.

He stood a full head taller than myself, lean to the point of appearing chronically malnourished, with the pronounced cheek and collar bones of an anorexic model or smack-raddled junkie, though with an altogether healthier pallor. And with a glint in his eye inferring access to untold forbidden means of recreation. An alluringly arcane squint to his smile hinted at the possession of some clandestine sacrosanct experience and insouciant awareness lying somewhere beyond my comparative naivety.

'My favourite,' he remarked, knocking back the dregs of his *Estrella* and indicating the book Grace had splayed out on the table before her.

We didn't encounter him for a day or two after that, having spent those first sun-dappled days dipping in and out of Sa Tuna, Begur, Aiguablava, Tamariu, Llafranc and Calella de Palafrugell; snorkelling in aquamarine coves and sampling tapas of *chipirones, calamari, albóndigas, gambas al ajillo, boquerones, chorizo and pimientos de Padrón* washed down with *sangria* and *cerveza* at beachside cafes. We were living the longed-for antidote to that final year slog for our degrees prior to embarking on our respective careers.

Grace had drifted down from Skye. I'd swept up from Ayr. We'd collided at Glasgow Uni's Halls of Residence a year earlier when the first thing that struck me about her was her sing-song Inner Hebridean lilt. That and the way she tilted her head, finch-like, whenever she felt inclined to let slip a smile that lit up the universe like a field of sunflowers.

One evening, having dined on a dish of rice with spiny spider crab followed by the ubiquitous *crème catalan* at a beach front restaurant at L'Estartit, we embarked on a post-prandial stroll along the promenade to El Grielles. We wound up sipping *ratafia* in the secluded corner of a nightclub called *The Custard Beast*. It was there that we next encountered the barman. He was sitting at a nearby table amongst a boisterous crowd engaged in a passionate and voluble debate that, from where we sat, appeared to be permanently on the brink of erupting into violence.

He noticed us on his return journey from the bar bearing a precarious trayful of drinks. Having first weaved his way through the throng to deposit his beverages, he approached our table, introduced himself, and asked if he could buy us a refreshment. Within half an hour, a plan had been hatched and plotted and agreed to embark upon a whirlwind exploration of the Dalí Triangle, with, as our guide and host, Francisco.

It transpired that, in addition to his shifts as a barman, Francisco was an art student drop out. He was also an occasional actor in a street theatre group specialising in improv who had even served a stint as a body double in a couple of Pedro Almodóvar films. Other roles he played were a crisis actor and, throughout the peak summer tourism season, a busker. He was frequently found serenading unsuspecting al fresco diners along L'Estartit's main drag fringing the harbour of a balmy evening with his battered acoustic and occasional accompaniment on a rusty mouth organ to embellish renditions of familiar ballads culled from the classic American songbook of late sixties/early seventies west coast troubadours.

Late the following Monday morning, Francisco met us at the harbour and proposed we start at the apex of the Dalí Triangle.

Turning that last bend into the shadowy, lunar, black treacle bay at Portlligat felt like driving into the beating heart of a Dalí painting, such was its unsettling familiarity from countless canvases. The home, when we entered it, had sprouted arms and legs and morphed over decades like a living breathing organism from its original fisherman's hut womb into a labyrinthine squat squid structure. It swallowed neighbouring huts, clung to jagged rocks, and seemed to be simultaneously cramped and sprawling with long thin twisting corridor tentacles unfurling into spaces crammed with a multitude of objets d'art. All with orifices and apertures affording a fresh perspective framing the bay or courtyards or olive groves. Francisco assumed the role of an informed and informative guide. His readily apparent ease and familiarity with Portlligat enabled him to provide a running commentary to accompany our mesmerised wander.

We then sped down to The Dalí Theatre Museum in Figueres and gorged on its abundant feast. Over-indulging on the surfeit of distracting images vying for attention, only the Mae West room had the desired impact. A whirlwind visit to the Gala Dalí Castle House in Púbol, infused with a muted medieval Moorish homage to the cult of Gala, proved less manic. A gentle coda to the Portlligat/Figueres mania.

That evening we lit a campfire on the beach. Francisco brought his guitar. Shedding inhibitions, steered by coy curiosity and appetite for experimentation to discard convention in favour of venturing forth to explore virgin territory, we sang three-part harmonies with gusto between wondering up at the star-filled sky, mesmerised by the waves lapping the shore. Entranced, Grace stripped and waded into the waves. The moonlight bathed her blue. Francisco and I followed suit.

So began our odyssey deep into the unknown. An exploration at times tentative, at others uninhibited. And brutal in its hungry intensity. I vowed never to forget that night of the Dalí Triangle summer when myself, Grace and Francisco came together to explore the glory of now.

two

pray for mariana

The gold-flecked leaves fluttered from barren branches to muffle and coat the concrete and tarmac at a time in our lives when we still worked to live rather than lived to work. We woke to a radio news bulletin about a bomb attack against the court building in Figueres by an armed Catalan nationalist separatist organisation.

Grace called Francisco for reassurance that he'd not been in the vicinity of Figueres at the time of the explosion. Her calls went unanswered. They remained unanswered over the next few days. Grace phoned at ever more frequent intervals. Her anxiety multiplied cumulatively with each unanswered call. She filled the vacuum of non-communication with an assortment of morbidly lurid scenarios. Mid-morning on a dreich Saturday, she eventually managed to contact Francisco. It was apparent immediately from his flat tone rather than anything he said that, despite his insistence to the contrary, something was amiss. It would be another few days and phone calls later before he let slip snippets about what had happened.

He *had* been in Figueres that day. And he hadn't been alone. His parents and younger sister had accompanied him. The occasion was Mariana's eighteenth birthday. Francisco's present to her had been a family ticket to the Dalí Theatre Museum prior to his parent's booking a table for lunch at a nearby restaurant. In a punctured monotone, a tentative narrative punctuated by pregnant pauses spilled from his lips as he fought to assemble his fractured thoughts into words.

That morning, the family had strolled past the court building en route to the museum in a carefree and celebratory mood, Francisco and Mariana to the fore, their parents, arms linked as always, bringing up the rear, when the devastating detonation blew the quartet off its feet. Over the course of various strained phone calls, some rambling and protracted, perforated, fragmentary, muddled and opaque, all of which we braced ourselves for with the exchange of a fleeting glance before dialling his number, Francisco would at some juncture find himself circling round to describe the immediate aftermath of the explosion as '*surreal*'. And always with a muted note of surprise at finding himself once more in the discomfiting position of having to search afresh in vain for an adjective adequate to articulate a horror already segueing into abstraction.

He recounted gaining consciousness, face down on the pavement, unable to move. He lay still for some time. A pulsating droning reverberated around his head. He was reluctant to attempt to move a muscle until the suffocating burden pressing him down made it incumbent on him to seek to writhe from beneath it. But no sooner had he sought to shift his weight a fraction than a pain shot up from his left knee, through his groin and stabbed upwards into the pit of his stomach. A surging sense of claustrophobia crushing down on him outweighed the pain of movement. Stealing a deep breath, he fought to twist free from the weight he was to learn had shielded him from the full force of the blast.

When first responders to the bomb site noticed his movement and rushed to his assistance, Francisco discovered that the weight pinning him down was the bloodied body of his mother. Searching for his sister and father, he found the twisted corpse of his father forever frozen in a fatal attempt to screen Mariana from the explosion. Just as his mother had saved him. Like his mother, his father had turned himself into a shield. Though the injuries sustained by Mariana were critical.

~⌒~

The explosion resulted in eleven fatalities and a dozen more casualties. Francisco was hospitalised with concussion, a broken arm and leg, a punctured lung and various lacerations and contusions, before being released with strict instructions to rest and recuperate. Mariana remained in hospital in a coma, having sustained a traumatic brain injury.

After a protracted silence, at a loss for something to say beyond the usual banal condolences, Grace heard herself offer, 'If there's anything we can do to help, just let us know. Anything.'

Francisco thanked her and assured her he would. Then, as he was about to hang up, he whispered, 'Could you pray for Mariana?'

three

friend or faux
or
friend or foe?

In the days and weeks that followed, we prayed for Mariana. Eventually, our prayers were answered. Some months later we learned that she was discharged from hospital, though her life would never be the same. Her movement was reduced to slow motion. Her balance and co-ordination were no longer instinctive. Her left-hand side had been rendered weak as a consequence of the traumatic injuries sustained to the right side of her brain.

When one of our regular distressing telephone calls, always initiated by us, ended prematurely with Francisco unable to continue, having voiced exasperation about how he was expected to foot the medical bills and ongoing care for Mariana having already bankrupted himself with his parents' funeral costs, we, by unspoken mutual consent, agreed to send him what little we could afford. Thereafter we established a direct debit into which a modest financial sum would be deposited into his bank account on a monthly basis. Grace phoned him to advise him of our intentions, overriding his initial refusal of our charity to insist he accept assistance. Eventually, he agreed, with a solemn promise to refund us in full as soon as he was able. In turn, we undertook to visit him in Girona as soon as practicably possible.

A mortgage and Rose's birth intervened to postpone our visit indefinitely. We continued to take it in turns to phone Francisco every other week or so and, when it became progressively problematic for us to visit him, Grace suggested that we book him a return flight instead.

We were ready and waiting at the airport's arrivals gate to greet him, but were unprepared for the deterioration in his appearance since we'd last seen him. Gaunt, his eyes, sunken and troubled, were unable to meet our gaze for more than a moment. His hair lank, posture slouched, gait a shuffle, his words, once a spontaneous eruption giving voice to an inquisitive and keen intellect, rendered detached and perfunctory.

The visit was endured rather than savoured. How could we have expected it to have been otherwise? The atrocity he'd suffered had cast a long shadow over our treasured, now distant, memories of an eternal sunshine Dalí Triangle summer.

If Francisco did realise a modicum of solace during his visit, it was in brief interludes, wordless exchanges of fleeting glimpses between himself and Rose when we caught him, inadvertently, unable to deny the urge to acknowledge, if not reciprocate, the infant joy Rose sought to bestow upon him. Ultimately, though, I suspected he was as relieved as we were at the conclusion of his trip.

We arrived at a decision, separately and through unspoken consent, that it was easier to keep quiet, do nothing and let inertia run its natural course than to articulate or seek to summon the requisite energy to justify to ourselves an active stance we were both reluctant to enact, to keep Francisco at a distance. We rationalised that the post-atrocity Francisco was not the same person as the pre-atrocity being. And maybe, we had, over time, been guilty of allowing ourselves to indulge in an edited distortion of that Dalí Triangle summer. Already it had started to lose some of the lustre that had blinded us to the prospect of any doubts about its resilience. We assuaged our guilt by maintaining our regular calls and deposits. That was how things remained, in stasis, for weeks. Then months. Until events led to us resigning ourselves to the conclusion that

Francisco had been anything but frank.

That belated realisation arose when he committed a faux pas. When the first snag in the thread of lies he'd spent a lifetime spinning began to unravel, we were left asking ourselves for the first time whether he was a friend or faux, or friend or foe?

A neutral observer might have detected a degree of irony in the fact that the incident that precipitated the unreeling of his narrative thread was an alleged counterfeit scam within which he was an apparently unwitting participant. The whole messy affair began to unravel when he had sold at auction a Salvador Dalí signed and hand-numbered limited edition unframed lithograph print named *The Quest*, which had belonged to his father and which he put up for sale with great reluctance, or so he claimed, to help foot Mariana's mounting medical bills. It was only when the print's new owner, a rotund retired mid-West American businessman, sought to insure his acquisition that a fresh authentication was sought and a claim made that the lithograph was, in fact, a forgery. This led to Francisco's arrest for fraud. The case generated a degree of press coverage, as anything to do with Dalí tends to, with no small amount of column inches expended on exploring the unreliable terrain of the blurred boundary between what is and what is not real.

This boundary was clouded deliberately by Dalí himself. He reputedly signed numerous blank canvases for images to be added later by assistants. But given that it is common for works produced by an artist's studio to be executed by assistants acting under the aegis of the artist, the question hanging over whether *The Quest* lithograph constituted a forgery or a fake remains ambiguous. If Dalí had authorised an assistant to produce it, could it be considered a forgery? Or was it a fake if

Dalí supervised and (pre)signed the artwork without executing it himself?

While such questions raised arguments worthy of debate, the impression left on us by Francisco's arrest, like a stubborn stain that sullies a treasured memory, was of a dubious practise perpetrated by a charlatan.

It raised doubt over Francisco's judgement and reliability. Consequently, when he next broached the subject of our willingness to contribute to his legal expenses, after much handwringing and, having first secured Grace's blessing, letting him down as gently as we were able, I explained that it was with much regret that, on this occasion, we found ourselves unable to oblige. We heard nothing from him for some time after that. But when we did, it became apparent immediately that the basis upon which our relation had been forged had altered. Fundamentally.

The abrupt nature of the ex-communication had irked me and continued to do so over the succeeding days and weeks until, rather than leavening a sense of unease, over time my niggling reservations continued to gnaw at me and to coalesce, forming themselves gradually into something more solid and ominous. It was at this point that Grace enquired about the darkening of my demeanour. When I confessed that I'd been harbouring some secretive suspicions, albeit unsubstantiated, about Francisco's character, but initiated by something I couldn't quite pinpoint, though I suspected it had something to do with his deafening silence ever since we'd declined his last request for financial assistance, Grace demanded that I either dismiss my doubts forthwith or lend them some credence through the presentation of incontrovertible evidence. Until such time, she affirmed, she would be giving Francisco the benefit of the doubt which, she added rhetorically and in a tone which indicated that a response in the negative would be preposterous, was the very least we owed him.

But the mounting suspicions that plagued me meant that I found myself quite unable to give Francisco the benefit of the doubt. This, I would come to suspect, was one source of the fissure that was to fracture all that I had. And who I was. And who I'd become.

And so, I made a decision, which I kept to myself like a guilty secret, to make some discreet enquiries into Francisco's character and affairs. But before I began, any such proposed investigation was stalled at the starting line and postponed indefinitely with the realisation that I had no idea how or where to begin such an undertaking. Instead, I resigned myself to do nothing but stay alert until such time as luck or fate made its presence known. I was ready to react accordingly when the opportunity presented itself.

four

silent
torment

In the event, I didn't have long to wait until my suspicions were confirmed. It was a little after 6.30pm on a smirry Wednesday evening when my viewing displeasure was interrupted by the doorbell. Grace leapt from the sofa to check that Rose's slumber remained undisturbed while motioning and mouthing in exaggerated mime for me to answer the door. I found two plain clothed police officers standing on the doormat. There's something about the ill-fitting, well-worn two-piece suit and tired striped tie combo favoured by plain clothed police officers that renders the need for them to produce their IDs surplus to requirements. Nevertheless, that was exactly what they proceeded to do.

'Good evening sir,' said the nearest, most senior officer. His junior colleague hung in the background, avoiding making eye contact. 'My name's Detective Sergeant Anderson and this is my colleague Detective Constable Whittaker. You are Alexander Young?'

I confirmed my identity and enquired how I might be of assistance.

'D'you know Francisco García?'

I confirmed that I did.

'We'd like to ask you a few questions about Mr García,' said the DS. When I failed to pick up on his slight pause, he continued. 'Perhaps we could do so here. Or would you prefer to accompany us to the station?'

I apologised for my momentary delay in inviting the officers into my home. Ushering them through to the living room, I stage whispered that my daughter was asleep in the adjoining bedroom, from which Grace, on cue, exited on tiptoe. Following a round of hushed introductions, Grace, stifling a yawn, sought to flounce her bed-flattened hair surreptitiously, and enquired if our guests would care for a tea or coffee. The DS declined on behalf of himself and his DC before proceeding to explain the reason for his visit.

'We're hoping you might be able to assist us with our enquiries into the financial affairs of Mr García,' he started. He then proceeded to reassure Grace's anxiety, manifested by her interruption to enquire about Francisco's health, before brushing aside, with a polished and no doubt well-rehearsed performance of professionalism, her enquiry about the nature of the police investigation by requesting that she firstly tell him a little about the nature of her relationship with Mr García.

Grace flushed and flicked a glance in my direction. I took this as a signal to deflect attention from herself with a timely intervention.

'We were – we *are* – friends,' I faltered, then hesitated, as if this bald statement should be sufficient in itself to satisfy the DS's requirements. When Anderson made no attempt to fill the vacuum that followed, I resigned myself to the conclusion that my testimony of textbook banality might not be sufficient after all. Reluctantly, I realised I had no option but to elaborate. 'We met him when we were on holiday. In Costa Brava.'

And so, slowly, through judicious deployment of hesitation, the odd furrowed brow, raised eyebrow, encouraging nod underpinned by some gentle probing, Anderson proceeded to elicit a tangled narrative from Grace and my own stumbling utterances. DC Whittaker recorded abbreviated versions of our statements in his notebook.

'And when did you last see Mr García?'

'Several months ago,' I said.

After yet another pause, Anderson asked, 'Could you perhaps elucidate? Where did you meet? What was the nature of your meeting? What did you talk about?'

Grace interrupted, finally, offering me some respite from what was starting to feel like an interrogation.

'We last saw Francisco when we waved him goodbye at the airport at the culmination of his week-long visit. At our invitation,' she said.

'I see,' said Anderson. 'And did he reside with yourselves for the duration of his stay?'

'He did,' replied Grace, without hesitation, but with mounting impatience evident in her clipped tone.

'And that was the last time you saw Mr García?'

Grace nodded her confirmation.

'And when did you last *hear* from Mr García?'

This time her answer was not as immediate. Or definite. 'Oh, around a week or so ago?' she offered, directing her question to me for confirmation. I nodded.

'And what was the nature of your conversation?'

'Francisco had sought our assistance, in the form of a financial contribution towards his legal expenses in a recent court case,' I said, 'which I suspect you know all about.'

Anderson allowed himself the hint of a smile and a small nod at this remark. 'And were you able to assist?'

'No.'

Witnessing me floundering, Grace interjected. 'Are you now able to tell us the nature of your enquiries?'

Anderson sidestepped the question with one of his own. 'Can I first ask if you are aware of the existence of a monthly direct debit transferring funds from your joint account into his?'

'We are,' confirmed Grace. 'Can you please tell us what this is all about?'

'All in good time,' said the DS. 'Can you tell me the reason for this financial arrangement?'

It was then that I chose to step once more into the fray to explain that it was a means of helping Francisco meet the costs of his sister's ongoing healthcare requirements following the explosion in Figueres which had killed his parents and left Mariana with a traumatic brain injury.

'I take it you're aware of this incident?' I asked.

Ignoring this query, Anderson instead asked me to confirm the date and amount of the first deposit. When I eventually did so, after conferring with Grace, he nodded to his colleague to record the details.

'Now, let me explain the reason behind my questions,' he said. 'Yesterday morning I received a phone call from an Inspector Rodríguez of the Catalan Police Force in Girona, requesting assistance for an investigation he was conducting into the affairs of Francisco García – '

' – investigation? But the court case is over,' interrupted Grace. 'Francisco lost.'

'This investigation concerns a different matter,' replied Anderson, displaying admirable restraint. 'Spain, as you may or may not know, has a state-owned institution which provides compensation for terrorism losses funded directly from the government budget. Spanish legislation stipulates reparation scales for injuries, death and loss of income for victims of terrorism. And compensation can include a life-time monthly pay out.'

'And?' I asked, sounding more strident than intended.

'And two days ago, Inspector Rodríguez arrested a man who'd claimed €500,000 in compensation after posing as a victim of the bomb attack against the court building in Figueres. This same individual, it seems, also tricked various members of the public into donating money to an unauthorised fundraising initiative which he established to solicit donations for funeral costs and ongoing healthcare expenses.'

When this observation still failed to yield any response from us, Anderson proceeded to inform us, with a tact for which, in time, we'd be grateful, that the man in question was Francisco García.

A protracted lull ensued, during which Whittaker squirmed uncomfortably, pen-poised with eyes darting between myself, Grace, and his superior, before the latter finally opted to bring the stalemate to a conclusion.

'Does this news come as a surprise?'

I nodded a confirmation

'You had no knowledge of Mr García's fraud?'

'None.'

'And yourself?' Anderson addressed his question to Grace, who, fixated on her own left shoe, shook her head once, slowly and deliberately. Anderson had encountered the silent tactic before and knew that the only way to deal with it was to respond in kind. Rather than probe any further, he opted to sit and wait for Grace or myself to respond however we saw fit. It did not surprise him that it was myself whose nature most abhorred a vacuum and felt compelled to fill it.

'You don't suspect us of being in some way complicit in this fraud?'

'Are you saying that Mr García duped you?'

'I am. *We* are,' I corrected, glancing at Grace.

'I see,' said Anderson, before once more plunging the room into intolerable silence. Then, deciding that he could not justify this silent torment a moment longer, he thanked us for our co-operation before adding as an aside that he might require further clarification on some matters at a later date.

With Grace still rooted to the spot, it was left to me to escort the policemen from our home. It was as they were set to step over the threshold into the common stairwell when I raised the matter of the direct debit. Anderson released his now-familiar half-smile, revealing that he had anticipated this enquiry.

'Mr García's bank account has been frozen, pending further investigation. His bank, and yours, have been informed that there's an ongoing police investigation into suspected fraudulent activity. I expect that you'll hear from your bank in a day or so, but you may well wish to expedite matters by contacting them directly and cancelling the arrangement.'

'And is there any prospect of us recouping our funds, given that we are the innocent victims of a fraud?'

Again, Anderson smiled.

'There may well be,' he said. 'But first I have to conclude my investigations and determine beyond reasonable doubt that you are indeed, as you say, *innocent victims*.'

And with that he turned to go before swivelling back suddenly to add, as if it had just occurred to him that very moment, 'Oh, you may be interested to know; Francisco García's an only child who was raised from the age of five by his maternal grandmother in Girona following the death of his parents in a car crash two decades ago.'

Taking care to close the front door gently, I permitted myself a few deep breaths before returning to impart Anderson's bombshell. As I waited for her to finish the tumbler of water she was drinking, Grace raised her eyes to meet mine. Struck by their plea to be spared from the anticipated onslaught of self-flagellation, enraged recrimination or forensic post-mortem, I surprised myself with an instinctive decision to keep DS Anderson's revelation about Francisco's family affairs to myself. For the time being.

five

going
through
the motions

I spent the remainder of the evening alone re-treading mental footsteps in a monotonous circle of futility, mulling over the hoary old chestnut of whether anyone ever really knows anyone, unable to share my sense of unease with Grace, who, unable to endure the burden of the words left unspoken, had plumped for the easy option of an early night in the hope that the following morning would throw a more favourable light on matters. It didn't of course. It never does. Instead, the new day heralded the birth of a fresh sense of unease making its presence felt between myself and Grace. I knew she knew I was keeping something about Francisco from her. And I knew she'd never confront me about it directly, leaving the discontent to fester undisturbed. While Grace, having witnessed the depth of the humiliation I felt from falling victim to Francisco's deception, sought to assuage my sense of shame by arguing that an assumption of trust was a benign trait not to be discarded lightly, I castigated myself for my gullibility with all the fortitude of a flagellant driven by the mortification of his own flesh.

Despite my repeated protests to the contrary, Grace was convinced I blamed her for Francisco's deception. There seemed nothing I could say or do that would convince her otherwise. I consoled myself by indulging in a fantasy of flying to Girona to confront Francisco head on, tracking him down and taking him by surprise, cornering him; I, furious and threatening violence, demanding he attempt to justify his unjustifiable lies before I exacted a savage retribution and beat the true confession out of him; Francisco, bloodied and bruised and taken aback by my unexpected presence, cowering in terror at my vicious attack, pleading for mercy and offering up a craven apology that sought to convince me that he had somehow been coerced into perpetrating falsehood. In my fantasy I dismissed Francisco's meek defence and revelled in my violent revenge.

Even as I indulged this fantasy, I was conscious that I did so safe in the knowledge that I was incapable of acting upon it. Confrontation has always been anathema to me. The execution of an act of violence upon any individual, no matter if I suffered as a direct consequence of Francisco's betrayal and now regarded him as my sworn enemy, lay beyond the realms of my nature, regardless of the depthless reserves of ill will I now harboured against him. I despised myself; both for my inability to execute an act of violence and for the resentment I bore and stored as a poor substitute; lamenting the insight that, without the option of a cathartic release afforded by violence, my incapacity for viciousness condemned me to passive acceptance of a corrosive self-sabotage spreading its bitterness throughout my marrow.

And so, I sought to content myself with nursing my wrath and attempting to defuse the festering animosity with Grace – contradictory pursuits, it seems obvious now – though not quite so evident at the time. At least not to me.

From that point on, our relationship was reduced to little more than a sham. Grace and I were never again intimate after the visit to our home by Anderson and Whittaker. Since then, whenever I tried to touch her, she would recoil violently, as though the touch of my palm laid gently on her shoulder was like a branding iron yanked from a furnace to prod her tender flesh.

Towards our bitter end, in a malicious statement intended to demean and humiliate and wound and strip me of any sense of dignity, Grace screamed in my face that she'd been going through the motions for years. The fact that I could never really bring myself to believe that this was true, preferring instead to convince myself that it was merely a false claim hurled with the sole intent of causing maximum hurt, was, in itself, likely testament to its truth.

It took me much longer than it should have to twig that the water Grace gulped was vodka.

And slowly, she slipped into a muffled somnambulist state, overcome with dull lethargy, insomniac, irritable, consumed by self-loathing for days dragging into weeks dragging into months on end. All that I could live with. Or so I told myself. What most disturbed me was her negligence of Rose. The transference of the provision of Rose's primary care from Grace to myself was not seamless. It was essential. Grace was no longer capable of assuming principal responsibility for Rose's care. I had lost faith in her ability to do so.

And then weeks on end of lethargy would be punctuated irregularly by exhausting weekend manic episodes of an exuberance as buoyant as a balloon inflated to bursting point before being let go to deflate in a reckless raspberry display of soaring and swooping, topsy turvy, higgledy-piggledy Catherine wheel death rattles, collapsing into a flat, slack, airless patch of primary coloured latex, limp and lifeless and appealing as a used condom.

Choosing my moment cautiously, having learned through trial and error when best to broach the subject, when she was placated and adequately lucid, though without sufficient strength to sustain a convincing argument to the contrary, I drew from her a resigned acceptance to attend the consultation with our GP I had prearranged for her. Having attended a series of these consultations, Grace was prescribed medication that, over a period of weeks, drew her back from the brink of the black blankness that had threatened constantly to envelop her and we were able to approximate a modicum of normalcy. For a while.

That approximation concluded abruptly when I arrived home one evening, fatigued following a stressful back shift, to encounter an angry mob of neighbours gathered in the common stairwell, banging on my door and ringing the doorbell repeatedly in a cacophonous chorus for Grace to let them enter. Inside, Grace's frantic yelling in demented rage at Rose was matched by Rose's inconsolable, desperately distressed cries for release from this hell. I brushed the neighbours aside and barged in, rushing to Rose's rescue. Naked, soiled and distraught beyond reason, I bundled her in my arms and stormed back out the door. I drove Rose straight to the safety of my mum's house without so much as a backward glance at Grace.

Rose safely deposited, I returned home to confront Grace. Instead, I confronted a vacant flat. Grace had abandoned us without a forwarding address. On a note she had pinned to the fridge with the souvenir magnet, a crass mass-produced travesty of a miniature melting clock replicating Dalí's *The Persistence of Memory*, she had scrawled '*I love Rose, but I can't trust myself to care for her anymore.*'. She proceeded to accuse me of stifling and suppressing her through a constant drip feed draining of her free will to live.

It was not until the following morning, as I sought to appease my agitation by tidying the flat, that I stumbled across her supply of antipsychotic medication discarded in the bathroom bin. Unopened.

Unable to cope with the immediate predicament of how to arrange and juggle the day-to-day practicalities of the provision of care for Rose while holding down my job, I depended on my mum for help, lying to myself that this was strictly a temporary measure until such time as I found a moment to stop and catch my breath and put some practical arrangements in place that would enable me to contrive a more satisfactory plan. I was conscious, though, that the perpetual postponement of these impractical arrangements would mean that the temporary measures would inevitably begin to assume a dull lustre of permanence.

⌣⌣

Having disappeared from our lives without warning, Grace made no attempt to contact myself or Rose. Until one morning many months later. I'd decided at the outset that it was her prerogative to initiate the reopening of any channels of communication and I fully expected her to do so, even when the days then weeks then months ebbed by. And when it finally dawned on me that she might never make contact, even then my reluctance to be seen to make the first move prevented me from doing so, as if being seen to do so would be tantamount to an admission of weakness that could be held against me as evidence in some obscure court at some obscure future date and mean that I had blinked first in some obscure game of chicken.

And even when, sometime after her disappearance, it occurred to me that, other than the scribbled note pinned to the fridge door, I had no evidence that she'd left of her own volition, even then, while I desperately conjured such fantastical scenarios, my reluctance to make contact, the attraction of the easy option, outweighed my desire for truth and remorse at her departure. So, when Grace finally did make contact, after all that time, I heaved a sigh of relief at the confirmation that she was alive. Acknowledging my surprise at my sense of release, I recognised that there may well be a residual of sentiment towards her lurking like a stubborn layer of sediment somewhere deep within my bowels.

Grace declared a desire to meet.

'Why?' I asked. 'And why now?'

'I'd prefer to explain in person,' she said, her voice sounding like Grace of old.

After torturing her with a deliberate hesitation before deigning to answer, I proposed a time and place. Grace agreed to my proposition before hanging up, pipping me right at the death once more in her game of one-upmanship. Or so it seemed to me. And so, we arranged to meet the next day at The Space Bar, Grace's favoured Merchant City haunt.

six

paper roses

Grace didn't even bother to leave me lingering for longer than ten minutes. Just long enough for me to ponder needlessly before resigning myself to my usual americano and lose myself in a tear-filled ode to self-pity from way back spilling from a tinny speaker perched precariously on an overhead shelf stacked with an abundance of chipped and cracked crockery teetering above an art deco scarlet and chrome steampunk *Gaggia* coffee machine.

I realise the way your eyes deceive me
With tender looks that I mistook for love
So take away the flowers that you gave me
And send the kind that you remind me of

As she prepared my order, the starch-aproned, pony-tailed, perfect-skinned slip-of-a-thing barista with the Manga nose and a waist the circumference of one of the dainty saucers threatening to crash at any given moment to the tiled floor from the shelf above, hummed a muted harmony as sympathetic counterpoint to the maudlin melody, rapt in her own melancholic reverie of a heartbreak of which appearances suggested she was far too young to have experienced...

Paper roses, paper roses,
Oh how real those roses seem to be
But they're only imitation
Like your imitation love for me

...and as the refrain faded, Grace appeared as if on cue. Temporarily thrown on re-encountering those alluring windows to the soul lightening her countenance, I had to fight to forget the abundance of shared memories from bubbling back to the surface from the sublimated depths into which I'd consigned them and hang on to the memory of the bitter distaste of its sour finale. Then, with her order taken and guarded greetings and insincere platitudes and pleasantries duly exchanged, with a casual throwaway ruthlessness, Grace nipped in the bud an anticipated lurch into an expanding universe of silence with her opening gambit.

'Rose's not your child,' she said. 'Before you ask, I'm not telling you who her father is.' She delivered her revelation with a throwaway insouciance, detonating her bombshell in a furtive pre-planned manoeuvre with the evident intent of inflicting a critical injury at an unguarded moment of vulnerability.

Vulnerability, I vowed, would be the last thing I'd reveal to her. Instead, I scrambled to construct an expression that suggested she'd informed me of nothing I didn't know already and that, even if I hadn't known already, couldn't care less about. As if responding robotically to a latent instinct of self-preservation, I grabbed automatically as a tactic of deflection as a kneejerk reaction.

'Are you her mother?'

'I am.'

'So am I. *And* her father. Regardless of what you might say. There's more to parenthood than biology.'

Grace's non-reaction led me to conclude that my attempted tactic of deflection had failed. It was at this juncture that the size six barista sidled over to deliver Grace's cappuccino, her cordiality plummeting as she skirted the fringes of the hostile environment within which Grace and I had only just reconstructed to cocoon ourselves within. The barista beat a hasty retreat as inconspicuously as she was able.

'I've a proposition for you,' said Grace. 'You remember Francisco?' she asked, stirring her coffee.

'Rose's father?'

The stirring stopped abruptly as the discarded teaspoon clattered against the rim of Grace's cup. The glare she threw me stopped time and cast me adrift in an eternity of contempt.

'He's an imposter,' she hissed.

'Tell me something I don't know already.'

She sighed.

'I doubt you'll remember, but when we first met him, he mentioned he was a part-time crisis actor. He and his cabal of freelancers were hired to act as fake victims of fake tragedies for various odd job military or police training exercises. Well, at some point Francisco had the ingenious idea – at least he claimed it as his own – of redefining the concept of a crisis actor. Instead of acting as fake victims of fake tragedies, his troupe would act as fake victims of *real* tragedies.'

This time she had my attention.

'I've been doing some digging and it transpires that he's a member of a clandestine cabal of mercenaries calling itself The Amino, bankrolled by whichever party or protest group has pockets deep enough to fund its members to pose as traumatised survivors of terrorist atrocities, distraught sufferers of racist rampages, distressed casualties of corrupt police shootings, sex crimes and other headline-grabbing incidents to secure maximum media exposure to manipulate public sentiment through blanket coverage of manufactured sob stories custom-designed to suit the pursuit of certain political agendas.

'Ironically, it's the very fact that, rather than some dark underworld overlord Svengali, such covert Machiavellian tactics are being adopted by liberal campaign groups in pursuit of policies designed to appeal to the bleeding heart liberal demographic – stricter gun controls, pro-choice, death penalty abolition, anti-fascist, equal rights and suchlike – that's enabled such subterfuge to flourish uninhibited while remaining under the radar courtesy of a cash-strapped, compliant, largely lethargic and sycophantic, sympathetic, servile media. But I can see that you're already starting to wonder if I'm some kind of deluded conspiracist.'

I didn't deny it. Instead, I reminded her that she'd mentioned she had a proposition for me.

'I do,' she said. 'I want you to pen an exposé on The Amino.'

'But, as you well know, unless you've forgotten, I'm a self-confessed bleeding-heart liberal myself and proud of it,' I reminded her. 'As are you. Unless I've never really known you.'

'You've known me,' she conceded. It was a sole note of conciliation sticking out like an obstinate shard through a fissure in the uniform sheen of her shield of nonchalance.

'So why would I seek to undermine the very campaigns I support? And why would you ask me to?'

'You wouldn't. But I know you. You like to think of yourself as a principled, altruistic kinda guy. You believe in truth and the pursuit of truth. And The Amino aren't bleeding heart liberals. They're mercenaries with a loyalty solely to their wallets. And here's the thing: your beloved liberal campaigners might not even be aware of The Amino's existence.'

'I thought you said they bankrolled them.'

'I did – because that's what my preliminary research led me to believe. But now I'm not so sure.'

'Why?'

'At the moment it's not much more than a hunch. But my suspicion is that it is, in fact, some murky Machiavellian mogul motherfucker – or band of motherfuckers (whose identity as yet remains obscure) – masterminding the whole mission; manipulating, manoeuvring and, ultimately, funding The Amino under the guise of an intricate web of shady offshore shell companies to make it appear that it's the liberal campaigners that have hired The Amino in order to discredit and undermine their positions.'

I was surprised by Grace's casual deployment of expletives. In my experience, she only swore under extreme duress.

'That's quite an intricate web of deceit you've woven for yourself there,' I said. 'On what basis are your suspicions founded?'

'It *is* intricate. And it'll take some time and methodical work to unravel. But after some investigation, carried out in my spare time to satisfy my own curiosity, I managed to convince my producer to give me some leeway to develop the idea further. But that was before the latest round of budget cuts started to hit and the deeper I looked into it, the more intricate the web grew and the murkier it seemed to get and the end result became less distinct until it reached a point where it looked less and less likely that I'd be able to deliver sufficiently conclusive newsworthy evidence within a realistically practical and imminent timeframe so that various other less interesting projects started to assume a greater priority. Resources were pulled and stretched and placed elsewhere – you know the score – and a decision had to be taken, finally, unavoidably, inevitably, that, if my investigations were ever to be green lit, some kind of external assistance would be required to bolster my suspicions with a damning revelation sufficient to deliver a breakthrough in the investigation.'

'That's all fascinating stuff,' I said. 'But what makes you think that I could be of any assistance, or would *want* to help? I don't know if you've heard or not, but I'm an arts correspondent juggling my work with life as a single parent. I'm neither an investigative reporter, a crime reporter, political or business correspondent, so I don't really see why you might think that I'm the best person to approach about this. And even if I was, why should I help you? Why should I care?'

'I know you've got no interest in helping me,' she said. 'I understand that. But this is a paid gig. The budget's tight, but I have a budget. And, if the end result's as explosive as I suspect it could be, it could be a game-changer in terms of your career –'

' – *Our* careers,' I interjected.

'Don't forget, I know how ambitious you are, or at least were,' continued Grace, as if oblivious to my interruption. 'I know you. I know very well that you're an arts correspondent. But I'm quite sure you know more than your fair share of helpful hacks upon whom you could call to help you out if need be as and when necessary. But they might not *be* necessary. And I know that you're most likely already suffocating in the vacuous vacuum of racing against the clock of the spinning hamster wheel of ever-tighter deadlines to file daily reports on the latest round of funding cuts to the arts, the most recent bureaucratic shambles at the universally derided and despised name-changing, shape-shifting arts sector quango, the endless shifting of deckchairs on the Titanic within the so-called 'creative economy', not to mention the latest exhibition from some uncritically-lauded-to-the-heavens celebrity mediocre wannabe controversialist fad conceptual artist, the perennial campaign to bail out the national theatre or ballet company or orchestra from the brink of bankruptcy year in year out ad nauseum yada yada.

'This could be your ticket to something more interesting and, well, worthwhile and meaningful. But mostly because it's personal to you. Francisco betrayed you. And me. The fact that you might help me out while nailing Francisco's an unfortunate by-product. This could be your chance to exact revenge, earn some money in the process, and with the prospect of being at the centre of a far bigger story the tentacles of which stretch across business, political and geographic borders.'

'So, you're appealing to my base instincts,' I said.

Grace's reply was an exasperated sigh.

'You say that the Beeb's budget's been cut,' I continued. 'D'you really think that The Herald has the resources to devote to research into a topic, the news value of which, if any, remains dubious? As does the timeframe?'

'If we collaborate; then maybe, yes I do,' said Grace. 'If The Herald secures the exclusive on breaking the story and the rights to run coverage in the run up to our broadcast, then it could work for both parties. Look, all I ask is that you take a quick glance at this and, if you think it might be of some interest, let me know. If not, I'll take it elsewhere and we'll part as enemies.'

When I failed to respond immediately, Grace took the opportunity to extract from the familiar leather satchel I'd bought her some years ago in Begur, a thin dossier. The coffee-stained, dog-eared cover page read, '*Fake Flowers, an exposé*'.

'Why *Fake Flowers*?' I asked.

'Because,' she said, 'I discovered that, when on a mission, The Amino identify themselves to each other by discreet rose gold fabric flowers pinned to their lapels.'

'Quaint.'

'Maybe. But underestimate them at your peril. These guys have no moral compass. They're *are* perfectly capable of committing the most depraved crimes against humanity for the right price in an instant. Untroubled. With no consideration of potential complications to a non-existent conscience.'

'You mentioned that, even without any investigative, political or business story experience, I might not need to seek out the help of my fellow members of Her Majesty's Press Corps. How come?'

'Take a look at this,' she said, flicking open the dossier to reveal a page torn from the programme for the imminent Edinburgh Festival Fringe. She pointed to an entry which read:

Kissing the Flower

Theatre (*stylish fast-paced post-modern tragi-comic homage to the Golden Age of Hollywood via the bastard lovechild of Alfred Hitchcock and Orson Welles*)

Venue 6, C Venues – C royale – studio 2,

Aug 4-18, 18:55

50 minute

Suitability: 16+ (Guideline)

Group: The Amino

This premiere tells the charming story of spies and broken-

hearted double-dealers. When hero Henri Harrington falls for chanteuse Lois DeLillo, the tale of her kidnapping, escape and eventual rescue will leave its audience desperate to discover if true love conquers all.

'Did you notice the name of the theatre group?' she asked.

'I did. You think this is Francisco?'

'I do.'

'You don't think it could be coincidental?'

'It could be. But then there's the matter of the playwright's name.'

'Ian Thome?'

Grace nodded.

'That's an alias used previously by Francisco. I think he's coming to Edinburgh under the guise of this play, hiding himself in plain sight to distract from his real intent – '

'Which is?'

'That I don't know. Yet.'

'And I don't suppose you've anything concrete to back-up your suspicions?'

'Nothing – other than the pattern of behaviour emerging slowly page by page within this dossier to coalesce into a fully blown portrait of terror in technicolour.'

'Well, not having perused it as yet, I'm not in a position to comment on his supposed pattern of behaviour beyond what I know already. But, for the sake of conjecture, let's assume that I'm interested in finding out if there's any substance to your suspicions. What next?'

'I want you to arrange an interview with Ian Thome about *Kissing the Flower* under the pretext of writing a preview. But really to see if you can shed any light on his true intentions.'

'But Francisco knows me so my presence would immediately alert him to the fact we're onto him.'

'That might not be a problem.'

'Why's that?'

Grace turned a page on her dossier to reveal a translation of a brief obituary from *El País* dated two days previously.

OBITUARY

Francisco García
Fraudster
Born: 11.02.90
Died: 25.07.20

Francisco García, who has been killed by his own hand when an Improvised Explosive Device he had seemingly intended to detonate on La Rambla, Barcelona exploded prematurely in his garage, was a notorious fraudster convicted for his part in a counterfeit scam involving the sale of a fake Salvador Dali lithograph which, he had claimed, had belonged to his father and which he put up for sale to pay the medical bills for his sister, an alleged survivor of a bomb attack against the court building in Figueres some years ago which, claimed García, killed his parents and left his sister Mariana with a serious head injury.

In fact, while that bomb did result in eleven fatalities, subsequent investigations into García's claim proved that he had posed as a victim of the attack in order to claim compensation. It transpired further that he had duped various members of the public into donating monies to a bogus fundraising initiative ostensibly to cover funeral expenses and ongoing healthcare bills.

Further investigation uncovered that, in fact, Francisco García was an only child who had been raised from the age of five by his maternal grandmother in Girona following the death of his parents in a car crash in the 1990s and rumours have emerged that he might even have been implicated in the Figueres explosion, though an ongoing police investigation into this incident has yet to deliver any firm evidence to that effect.

'I'm confused. How am I supposed to extract my revenge on a dead man?'

'That would be difficult,' admitted Grace. 'But I'm not convinced he's dead.'

'Oh?'

'Take a look at this,' she said, leaning closer to show me her smartphone. The familiar scent of *Chanel No 5* resurrected a multitude of suppressed memories as she did so. Grace clicked on a saved icon before zooming in on a blurred CCTV image of a bearded man in a skip cap, Ray-Bans, jeans, blank white tee, and black backpack passing through passport control at Girona Airport. The footage was date-stamped the day before the day before. 'I believe that's Francisco, en route to Edinburgh.'

'Where'd you get this?'

'I have my sources. And like any good journalist, they're confidential.'

'That's a very blurry image,' I said. 'How can you be sure that's Francisco? Was his name on the passenger list?'

'No. But *Ian Thome* was.'

'And you're convinced he's in Edinburgh on illegitimate business?'

'I *do.*'

'Then is this not a matter for the police? Don't you think you should inform that policeman who questioned us about Francisco – Anderson – about your findings?'

'I have done.'

'And?'

'And nothing. He indicated that he required something concrete before he could take the matter any further. That's where you come in.'

'Which takes me back to my original point: my presence would immediately place Francisco on alert.'

'It would. But we're running out of options. And time. I can't go into detail as yet, but I think that whatever he's planning – and whatever it is it won't be pleasant – is imminent.'

I pondered this for a moment before proceeding.

'You said earlier that you suspected the end result of any investigation could be explosive. What did you mean?'

'I meant it literally. In addition to Francisco's idea of redefining the concept of a crisis actor from acting as fake victims of fake tragedies to fake victims of *real* tragedies, I believe he's taken the concept a stage further still. Rather than acting as guns for hire, The Amino's taken control of its affairs for itself.'

'How?'

'By instigating the tragedies.'

'So, The Amino are the murderous Machiavellian motherfuckers?'

'And Francisco's the ringleader. The head honcho. The main *muthafucka,*' she said.

'Well, that's some pet theory. And, if true, it sounds way too dangerous for me to get caught up in,' I deadpanned.

'Sandy,' said Grace, changing her tactic unsubtly with a radical new line of attack. 'D'you think this is easy for me? Coming to you like this? Pleading for your help? It's the *last* thing I want to do!'

I remained intent on ignoring the sympathy card she'd dealt and proceeded to wave under my nose. Resigned to the ineffectiveness of her plea for pity, Grace observed:

'You didn't appear too surprised to read in Francisco's supposed obituary that he was an only child. You knew that already, didn't you?'

I considered denying any prior knowledge for a moment before deciding, on balance, to answer in the affirmative.

'How long have you known?' she probed.

'DS Anderson informed me that evening he came 'round asking questions about Francisco.'

'And you didn't tell me?'

'You were upset. I didn't want to add to your distress.'

'How considerate of you,' she said.

∼∽∽

I exited The Spacebar under a cloud of culpability with the dossier in my hand. That evening, unable to resist the temptation, I pored over it in detail. The Amino, Grace conjectured in numerous footnotes and asides scribbled hastily on yellow Post-it Notes stuck to the margins of underlined and highlighted passages on page after page, comprised between four and six like-minded anarcho terrorist mercenary vigilantes. Each member had his or her own specialist skill set. This ranged from supremely sophisticated hacking proficiencies to hand-to-hand combat, survival and military experience. Combined with periodic exposure and insight into the highest echelons of the secret service, these talents created a spooks-gone-rogue talent for spying and duplicity, forming a cadre with an appetite for extreme violence. With no compunction about the commitment of heinous crimes in the relentless pursuit of its aims to sow seeds of chaos and confusion and destruction for the right price. And, what's more, it seemed that Grace had even uncovered The Amino's credo. What she coined its *hypocritic* oath – to which members swore allegiance and which she claimed was tattooed across their left biceps.

Say one thing, do the opposite.

As I sat there, pen in one hand, fork poised in the other, waiting for the microwave to ping so that I could tuck into my regular Tuesday night ready meal before Rose started crying for her bedtime story, I confessed to being intrigued by the tale contained within the dossier. I conceded that Grace was right about me being bored with my job. Reflecting on that disorientating spiralling conversation in The Spacebar, I wound up just about convincing myself that there was surely nothing to lose from poking around to see what, if anything, I might discover about the mysterious Francisco García. It would certainly beat waking befuddled to find myself drooling and slumped on the sofa having overdosed yet again on weekday early evening reality TV.

But instead of searching aimlessly for some incriminating background material on Francisco, following some elementary online research, I ordered myself a paternity test kit.

seven

the
opposite

The first thing I did at my desk the following morning was phone the Fringe Press Office, reserve a seat at the press preview of *Kissing the Flower* that evening and book a slot for a press interview with Francisco in a coffee house adjacent to the theatre as soon as the curtain fell.

I decided to play it straight – if you can call contriving the pretence that we'd never met before and therefore had no history, no shared friendship, no grudges or grievances to bear as 'straight'. I introduced myself to Francisco as if to a stranger. For his part, he registered not a flicker of recognition when we met, which meant that the longer the interview went on with neither of us willing to break the pretence of unrecognition, the more uneasy I felt. Either Francisco was an exceptionally good actor – if I didn't know I knew him, there was no way I would have known I'd known him – or he really *had* deleted me from his memory banks. I castigated myself for having initiated the charade. How might Francisco have responded had I not done so? Might he have offered an apology or even some plausible explanation for how things transpired and misfired? While on constant alert for him letting slip an inadvertent comment that revealed our shared past, I had to fight a mounting temptation to do so myself. It was disconcerting, leading me to doubt my memory of events and threatening to crack the surface of the past I'd constructed so solidly and unquestioningly for myself.

'Tell me about how *Kissing The Flower* came about,' I asked.

'I suppose it was the confluence of various influences that happened to be swirling around in the ether at the time,' Francisco began. 'It was around nine months or so ago when, over the course of a lost weekend, I reacquainted myself with *Citizen Kane* for the first time in many years, followed by a couple of Hitchcocks – *Vertigo* and *To Catch a Thief* – while I was reading Fitzgerald's *Tender is the Night*. I found myself … well, I found myself inspired by something. Something I can't quite define with any precision. But some idea lurking at the core of these fictions that opened the door to a consideration of matters of fact in a different room with a different view to that which I'd been used to observing previously. I felt inspired to pay homage to them by having a stab at creating a fictional universe for myself to inhabit.'

Although this response sparked a glimmer of a memory of a conversation we'd had in L'Estartit when we'd discussed some of our favourite books and films, his words and gestures betrayed not the slightest indication that this memory was rooted in reality.

'It's quite an intricate, fast-moving plot. Did the whole thing come to you in a flash of inspiration fully realised – '

' – I wish – '

' – or develop as you went along?'

'Blood sweat and tears! The plot developed painstakingly, laboriously, though I'm gratified if, as you say, it succeeds in giving the illusion, in parts, of being fleet of foot. I wanted to keep things on the move. Quite deliberately. Briskly. And sometimes brusquely.'

'Indeed. The language used on occasion seems deliberately forthright and abrupt – '

'Fuck yeah. If not downright offensive.'

'Indeed. The main characters seem for the most part to be on the offense rather than the defence and revel in causing umbrage through industrial language. Was this a conscious decision?'

'Yes and no. Truth be told; the characters tend to speak how I speak. And I've been told more than once that I'm an offensive character.'

'Well, let's talk about your character. *Kissing The Flower*'s your debut. Tell us a little bit about yourself. What's *your* story?'

Francisco proceeded to trot out a well-rehearsed and, I was convinced, entirely spurious mini autobiography sketching out a childhood of high jinks and laying low in Miami, teenage years spent fluctuating between periods of existential angst and erotic agitation interspersed with frenetic outbursts of energetic aggravation in New York followed by an extended itinerant period passed listlessly, aimlessly bumming his way around Europe prior to winding up most recently in London's East End. Rather than probe and question the authenticity of this engaging memoir, I opted instead to brush over it. I proceeded with the interview while accepting the unwritten rules of our charade; to refrain from attempting to unmask Francisco's true identity and, all the while, furtively sought to gain any insights that might verify Grace's suspicions about his and his groups' nefarious intent.

And so, the interview proceeded in a playful cat and mouse game of catch me if you can, ostensibly chatting around and chancing upon the various literary themes and theatrical tropes raised by *Kissing The Flower* on the surface, even as, all the while, seeking to trip up Francisco and trap him with an unintended revelatory glimpse into the murky depths of a hidden agenda of darker undercurrents. While I enjoyed the ping pong tête-à-tête, there came a point when I found myself unable to resist the temptation to poke Francisco with a sharp stick to see if I might prick his shield of unrecognition.

'It's not unknown for a writer's first efforts to contain an autobiographical element. *Kissing the Flower* is your debut: what does it reveal about you?'

'Hopefully little. If any autobiographical details have crept into the script, they've done so inadvertently.'

'It seems to me that your male lead, Lachlan Urquhart, a self-made man of independent means is, at heart, a tragi-comic character betraying symptoms of having suffered from direct exposure to imposter syndrome, if anything the very opposite personality traits of Henri Harrington, the nom de plume and persona he adopts, whose ethos appears to be '*say one thing, do the opposite*' – ' Francisco betrayed not so much as a flicker of recognition or unease at this casual mention of The Amino's supposed credo – 'was that your intention?'

'I think you might be reading too much into it.'

This evasiveness alerted me to the fact I may be onto something. I pressed the point home.

'So, the internal conflict I've read into your lead character exists only in my imagination rather than an element of drama you'd written into the script?'

'It was perhaps alluded to in the script. But I think I'd have to credit Gabriel Gardener with developing it to the point that you suggest it's apparent. It's not something I'd added consciously.'

At that moment, smelling blood, I changed tack and sprung an impromptu attack.

'Are you familiar with the work of Salvador Dalí?' I asked.

'Not particularly,' shrugged Francisco.

My supposed inquisition was parried and dismissed effortlessly by a shrug and a curled lip. Francisco's shield, it seemed, was impenetrable while my frail pretence of unrecognition was laid bare for him to trample over triumphantly. But rather than doing so, Francisco refrained from treating me with open contempt, opting instead to leave me to stew in the juices of my own incompetent and impatient tempestuousness as he guided me back to the comfort of the charade of unfamiliarity for the remainder of the mock interview.

As we parted, Francisco initiated a handshake and, grasping my opportunity, I took his hand and, leaning closer as if to impart information of an extremely sensitive nature in confidence, stage-whispered in his ear, 'Grace sends her regards.'

Once again Francisco revealed not a flicker of recognition but instead freed himself effortlessly from my would-be vice-like grip with a flick of his wrist, threw me a look of exquisite condescension and turned on his heels. I waited till he'd disappeared from view.

After a furtive glance over my shoulder, I took a paper napkin and, under the guise of stacking our dirty cups and saucers, slipped the teaspoon, which I'd watched Francisco use to scoop up the remaining foam from the dregs of his cappuccino, into a sealed polythene bag which I'd brought along for this express purpose, and pocketed it surreptitiously.

I phoned Grace that evening to inform her of my failure to elicit any insights from my interview with Francisco. Her silence spoke volumes.

'At least now we know he's alive,' I said, as much to fill the silence as anything.

"I knew that already,' she said, unwilling to throw me a crumb of comfort. Then, as if hearing the harshness in her voice, she altered her tone. 'Fortunately, I made some progress. I received an anonymous tip-off this afternoon.'

'And?'

'And I now know the target.'

'*And*?'

'And it's worse than I thought. *Much* worse.'

She refused to discuss the matter further over the phone but agreed to meet me at The Space Bar in the morning, consigning me to a sleepless night. In truth, her phone call was not the sole cause of my insomnia. I had other things on my mind.

The paternity test kit I'd ordered had arrived that morning. Having pored over the instructions, I swabbed Rose's cheek thoroughly prior to overseeing her brushing of teeth. Then, once she was tucked up in bed sound asleep, I swabbed the teaspoon I'd stolen from the café where I'd interviewed Francisco. I doubted that this DNA sample would suffice but had no option but to give it a go. If it worked, I'd know beyond doubt if Rose and Francisco have a biological relationship when I received the results back from the lab within the next two to three working days.

My glowing review of *Kissing the Flower* appeared in the paper the following morning.

eight

kissing
the flower

LA VIE EN ROSE:
KISSING THE FLOWER

by Sandy Young

You don't have to be a cunning linguist to hazard a guess at the sexual act for which the title of this play serves as a typically unsubtle metaphor.

There are heavy hints aplenty throughout this frolicking romp, given the numerous oblique allusions and multitude of nudge nudge wink wink references to Citizen Kane's Rosebud.

Yet while familiarity and fondness for Orson Welles' masterpiece, together with the oeuvre of Alfred Hitchcock will no doubt allow that element of the audience in the know to congratulate themselves on picking up on its plethora of references, the fast pace of this self-styled 'post-modern tragi-comic homage to the Golden Age of Hollywood' is positively brimming over with more than sufficient vim and vigour to stand on its own two feet.

Even as a constant stream of double entendres worthy of Finbarr Saunders whizz silently overhead to implode safely in some dim and distant Carry-On backwater far far away.

A cynic might yawn, scratch a psychosomatic itch absent-mindedly, nit-pick, quibble and aim the odd pot-shot at a yarn with an over-familiar foundation in a farrago of action adventure tropes with superficial lazy and shallow cyphers and stereotypes lifted straight from Central Casting before being woken from his semi-somnambulistic state by the crisp fresh delivery of some quick-witted ping-pong dialogue and some superlative performances which somehow unsuspectingly bring a juicy new perspective and breathe life and vitality into these stock cardboard cut-outs, giving them a pulse and the appearance of real flesh and blood and all the mess of humanity.

The triumph of this piece can be ascribed to the talent of its energetic and vivacious cast.

In particular, the two main leads who seem to bounce off each other (literally, on occasion), sending sparks of barely suppressed sexual desire shooting wildly off into the front rows as they revel in wringing every last morsel of nuance from this intricate, fast-paced script and twisty plot deploying sly satire interspersed with moments of frivolity sliced and diced on occasion with unexpected dramatic changes of pace and tone that strip away all the fun and frolics in a ferocious sweep of unsparing savagery to lay bare hidden reservoirs of dark and troubling depths and doubts to deliver an at times dazzling piece of theatre that resonates far beyond that which it really has any right to.

For all is not as it seems at first blush in Kissing the Flower.

This would-be derring-do tale of a fantastical bygone age of exotic espionage is populated by femmes fatales and louche lounge lizards, acrobatic aristos, cool clarinettists and anachronistic anarchists with a knowing nod and wink to contemporary audiences to underline and mock – sometimes fondly, sometimes cruelly – the many discomfiting disparities and surprise similarities between then and now ('plus ça change, plus c'est la même chose' as Henri Harrington reflects ruefully with a sigh, before downing his absinthe in a oner in one memorable scene) in a giddy spiral of a vertigo-inducing performance played to the max with gusto and gung-ho.

From its opening scene set on Paris's Left Bank, to the

soothing strains of Louis Armstrong's La Vie en rose lulling us into a reliably false sense of security, we are soon whisked away to the Côte d'Azur.

There, amidst a succession of scene-stealing cameos from a supporting cast hamming it up to the hilt with a series of skittish sketches of real-life hedonists – from the Fitzgeralds to Hemmingway, Valentino, Maurice Chevalier and Picasso – to blend sparkling fragments of real life to add lustre to this glittering adventure of romance and fortunes won, lost and faked.

Newcomer Gabriel Gardener assumes ownership of the male lead role of Henri Harrington, modelled evidently on the chisel-chinned, sleek haired To Catch a Thief-era Cary Grant, with all the athleticism and animal magnetism present and correct.

Opposite number and fellow newbie Liz Loganberry evidently made the casting director's day whenever she first sashayed across his stage to inhabit the essence of Lois DeLillo, the quintessential femme fatale with all her alluring blend of guile and vulnerability and promise of forbidden fruits, all dolled up to the nines but desperate to be unbuttoned with archetypal blood red stilettoes, jet black fishnets, ruby red lipstick and wayward strands of dyed blonde hair dangling over panda eyes alert with a dare and the eternal allure of the contradictory innocent come-on all present and correct as she blows ghostly blue smoke rings from her ever-present Gauloises into the spotlight while running rings round every male member of the entourage who meanders into her path with a flick of her fringe and her killer put-downs.

Attempting to summarise

this slippery, twisting and twisted plot without unravelling its many mysteries and ruining it for audiences by inadvertently spilling the spoilers is like being challenged to a wrestling match with a giant octopus with one hand while completing a Rubik's Cube against the clock with the other.

So, it is infinitely safer to point potential theatregoers in the direction of the blurb, which appears to have perfected the art of setting the scene and giving a flavour of what you might expect without saying anything much at all.

'When would-be lothario Henri Harrington, the nom de plume of Lachlan Urquhart, a seemingly self-made man of independent means, investigative journalist by day, jazz clarinettist by night, falls head over heels for femme fatale absinthe addict Lois DeLillo, dancer and occasional singer, not to mention runaway jewellery heiress, the helter skelter tale of her kidnapping, escape and eventual rescue will leave its audience desperate to discover if, as in all the best fairy tales, true love will conquer all.

'Are Henri and Lois destined to live happily ever after? Or will the dark shadow of reality make its presence known at the final curtain?'

Only a killjoy of the highest order would dare reveal the answer to that question in advance.

This reviewer is no killjoy (at least not of the highest order) so will refrain from doing so.

Instead, he will recommend that, regardless of your familiarity or ignorance of the films of Orson Welles or Arthur Hitchcock, should you have a penchant for suspense and intrigue, coupled with romance and adventure washed down with lashings of escapism topped off with a surprisingly incisive and insightful commentary on the zeitgeist as viewed initially through rose-tinted spectacles and latterly through a glass darkly, then you might well find yourself in for a cinematic, theatrical treat.

Particularly if you happen to be a cunning linguist with a penchant for Charles Mingus and cunnilingus.

nine

the
ends

No sooner had pleasantries been exchanged than Grace muttered distractedly, 'Francisco's planning some sort of explosion at the Tattoo,' as though some triviality barely worth mentioning had just popped into her head.

The prospect of this bombshell struck me as preposterous and obvious simultaneously. A despicable plan hatched from ingenious malevolence born out of a treacherous mind warped by a twisted logic.

'It makes a sick sense,' she said, articulating my thoughts. 'A military event with British Armed Forces, Commonwealth and international military bands and a thousand or so musicians, pipers, drummers, singers and dancers performing each night to an audience of 9,000 on the esplanade of Edinburgh Castle during the world's largest arts festival broadcast globally to up to 300 million people.

'And this year the BBC's due to broadcast the finale live. So it's hard to think of a more tempting target for a terrorist organisation in terms of the casualties it could inflict and the global media coverage such a devastating atrocity would garner.'

'How d'you know this?' I asked, still grappling to assimilate the full scale of this terrifying prospect.

'I told you. I have my sources,' she said.

'Have you informed the authorities?'

'I've reported what I know to the National Counter Terrorism Security Office and sent them a preview of tomorrow night's news report extracted from *Fake Flowers* to mull over. I'm not sure what they make of it all as yet. I don't think they know whether to treat it seriously or if they think I'm some kind of conspiracy theory crackpot. But I had to give it a shot.'

'Does your report name Francisco?'

Grace nodded.

'So, you're convinced about this. The threat's genuine and he's involved?'

'As I told NaCTSO, the Beeb's not in the habit of broadcasting material unless we've checked it out thoroughly in advance. I'm giving you the heads-up, as per our agreement, to offer *The Herald* first dibs on the exclusive, on the understanding that you flag up our news piece,' she said. 'The combined media coverage should exert pressure on NaCTSO to investigate the matter thoroughly. Who knows; with a bit of luck, between us we could wind up playing a part in averting a major terrorist atrocity.'

'To what end would he – would anyone – wish to carry out such an act?' I wondered aloud, still playing catch up, struggling to make sense of the nonsensical.

'Well, that's the question. When it comes to terrorists it's all about the ends. And the ends justify the means. Acts of terror are always a means to an end. But, as I've said, so far as I can tell, Francisco's Amino's an end in itself. It's only interest is in making money. So, the question is 'what's the end of whoever's paying The Amino to commit this atrocity?'. The answer to that as yet remains a mystery.'

'Both the motive and the identity of the paymaster?'

Grace nodded. 'Unsurprisingly, *Kissing the Flower* has already cancelled its Fringe run under the pretext of various cast members displaying symptoms of a flu-like virus … but you were questioning my conviction about Francisco's involvement. I take it you harbour some doubts?'

'I'm not sure what to believe,' I admitted. 'When I interviewed him it was if we'd never met before. There wasn't the slightest flicker of recognition. And that was disconcerting. It made me doubt that we *had* met.'

'But you're certain that the person you met yesterday was Francisco?'

'Of course. I'm just having a problem processing much beyond that.'

'Well, it's a problem you'll have to overcome sooner than later if *The Herald* wants an exclusive – we broadcast tomorrow evening.'

This was the kind of rare day I was supposed to relish. This should have been my dream scenario: the scoop of a story of potential national importance falling into my lap, placing me in the enviable and unique position on the inside track. And I was excited by the prospect this rapidly unfolding story offered. But I was also anxious about the pressure already mounting to produce intelligible copy to the deadline of a couple of hours hence if I managed to clear the first hurdle of convincing Kerr of its news value.

And penning this piece lay well beyond my comfort zone. Investigative reporting was not my forte. Spending an afternoon tracking down and pestering the bereaved parents of a teenage motorcyclist killed by a drunken driver for a quote was not my idea of fun. But give me a book or a film or a play to review; or an author, actor or director or playwright to interview, and I could guarantee delivery of a thousand words within an hour or so. I could produce running commentary and opinion on any type of popular artform at any time of the day or night without expending too much effort. But when it came to reporting real life, I hit a blank screen dead end.

Fortunately, or unfortunately for me, Kerr grasped the importance of the story immediately and instructed me to get onto it straightaway. While I was tempted to try to pass the buck onto Dick and Hill, my hard-nosed investigative colleagues, this proved not to be an option. They were already out and about following a lead on some sordid drug-related gangland turf war over in Edinburgh. So there was no escape route. I'd have to write the piece myself.

ten

front
page
lead

PLOT TO BLOW UP EDINBURGH CASTLE AT TATTOO
MANHUNT FOR MERCENARIES CENTRES ON CAPITAL

Exclusive by Sandy Young

A plot to blow up Edinburgh Castle at the height of the Royal Edinburgh Military Tattoo has been uncovered by BBC Scotland which will broadcast the findings of its investigation on Reporting Scotland BBC1 at 6.30pm tonight.

If it were to succeed unchallenged, it is estimated the planned explosion could result in the most devastating terrorist attack on British soil in modern times, with the loss of life estimated to number in the hundreds, if not thousands.

While the threat remains very much alive, the police are actively pursuing leads and have sought to reassure the public by stating their confidence in their ability to thwart the attack while simultaneously advising members of the public to be on the alert and to report any suspicious behaviour in or around the castle in the lead up to and during the Tattoo, which opens on Wednesday evening.

The ringleader of the little-known group behind the plot has been named as Francisco García, a Spanish national and a convicted fraudster whose death had been reported in his homeland only last week, but who, in fact, is believed to be alive and in Edinburgh where he was due to perform a run of shows with a theatre group.

That production, which has since been cancelled, is believed to have been a ruse designed to deflect attention from a plan to detonate a massive explosion at Edinburgh Castle during the Tattoo by a group called The Amino, thought to execute atrocities on behalf of various organisations before proceeding to pose as innocent victims to extract cash and secure media exposure to manipulate public sentiment and push certain agendas.

In the Reporting Scotland investigation Fake Flowers, reporter Grace Robertson reveals that García was formerly a member of A group of freelance Spanish crisis actors hired to act as fake victims of fake tragedies for various military and police training exercises. She claims that at some point García chose to act as a victim of real tragedies.

When on a mission, it is said that The Amino wear fake flowers pinned to lapels for identification purposes.

A recent edition of the Spanish newspaper El País ran an obituary of García which reported that he had been killed by his own hand when a bomb he had planned to detonate on La Rambla, Barcelona exploded prematurely.

The obituary described García as a notorious fraudster convicted for his part in a counterfeit scam involving the sale of a fake Salvador Dalí lithograph.

Fake Flowers contains footage of a man it identifies as García passing through passport control at Girona Airport last Thursday.

According to the documentary, The Amino comprises various anarcho terrorist mercenary vigilantes with a shared appetite for violence and no compunction about the commitment of atrocities for the right price.

Police Scotland has confirmed that it is investigating the

A recent edition of the Spanish newspaper El País ran an obituary of García which reported that he had been killed by his own hand when a bomb he had planned to detonate on La Rambla, Barcelona exploded prematurely.

The obituary described García as a notorious fraudster convicted for his part in a counterfeit scam involving the sale of a fake Salvador Dalí lithograph.

and, in a statement, said: 'Previous events have shown us that attacks can happen at any time or place without warning. Our priority is the safety and security of all those attending events and crowded places. The public can help us keep events and areas safe by being vigilant for anyone or anything that looks out of place or suspicious and reporting it to a member of staff, security or police.'

No details have been given about the suspected nature of the attack. Royal Edinburgh Military Tattoo Chief Executive, Brigadier Donald Allman, stated: 'We are presently working alongside the police and the National Counter Terrorism Security Office to ensure that we have all necessary security measures in place to counter any terrorist threat.

'While I would endorse police advice that members of the public be on the alert and report any suspicious behaviour in or around the castle in the lead up to and during the Tattoo, I am entirely confident that the threat will not be realised *and would urge ticket holders not to alter their plans but instead demonstrate that they will not be cowed by cowardly terrorist threats and join us in this tremendous extravaganza, which is increasingly recognised as the jewel in the crown of the world's largest arts festival.'*

eleven

imposter syndrome

The reaction was immediate. Within seconds of going online the story had generated a flurry of responses running the gamut of considered comment to outraged outpourings of reactionary venomous vomit all feeding off each other maniacally in their own viral cesspool surging, regurgitating, seamlessly, senselessly across international borders and timelines to be copied and pasted and poked and tweeted and emoticonned ad nauseum. By the time the printed version hit the newsstands, the buzz about the plot to blow up Edinburgh Castle had escalated from the front page of one broadsheet to a lead item on most broadcast and digital media internationally.

As I sat at my desk waiting for my computer to boot up, I'd already been inundated with multiple emails from a plethora of media folk urgently seeking contact numbers for further information clogging up my phone alongside countless voicemails requesting the same. I prayed that Grace's research would prove sufficiently robust to stand up to the intense scrutiny because should any dubiety surface about any of the claims made in her story they would surely be ruthlessly exposed by the ferocious and ravenous business of ferrets diving in to tear off a morsel of this juicy titbit of a story for themselves.

I was at my desk no more than quarter of an hour before a tweet from twitter handle @avidadollarsxxx posted the following comment to a link to the story...

This is fake news; a slanderous hoax concocted by a wannabe mediocre provincial journalist colluding with his BBC reporter wife to tarnish the name of an innocent man of whom they share an unfounded grudge with the sole purpose of advancing their stalled careers. Why have they not revealed their relationship with this supposed terrorist? #fakenews #slander #careeradvancement

I had no doubt about the identity of *@avidadollarsxxx.* I realised immediately that I had some explaining to do to Kerr but, before that, I had to warn Grace that we, ourselves, were at grave risk of becoming the story. I'd just lifted the receiver to give her the head's up when a large, newspaper ink-stained and calloused hand swooped from behind me, yanked the receiver from my grip and slammed it back in its cradle.

'My office. Now,' said Kerr.

Permanently harassed, Kerr had never been known to beat around the bush when he could simply bulldoze his way through it.

'What – the – fuck?' he started, momentarily lost for words. 'What the *fuck's* going on?'

I had just about managed a half shrug when he raised his right hand.

'Stop right there,' he said. 'You *know* this fucker?'

'Well – '

' – it's not a difficult question. Yes or no?'

'Well … yes.'

'And you neglected to mention that fact yesterday?'

'I wasn't quite sure of the relevance.'

'Oh, I *see*! What the … what the absolute fuck am I supposed to do now?'

And there I was. Paralysed. Caught in the unflinching glare of the spotlight. Centre stage. Stark naked before an audience of my peers with nowhere to hide. Ruthlessly exposed as the fraud I always knew myself to be. All my coping strategies and relaxation techniques for my omnipresent imposter syndrome were rendered redundant in an instant. I unspooled right there and then under Kerr's perpetual glower.

'Well?'

'I don't see why the fact I knew this guy's relevant. The story's about a possible terrorist attack – '

'Fuck the story! Why didn't you tell me you knew this fucker? Do you bear a grudge against him? Is this your way of fucking him around; by fucking *me* around? D'you stand by your story?'

'I do. I – '

'Well, you better be right 'cause if you're wrong – or if it turns out you're fucking me around – you'll be out that fucking door before you know what's hit you. Unemployed and unemployable with zero prospects for the foreseeable. I'll make it my life's mission to make certain of that. Sure as fuck I will. In the meantime, you're off the story. I'm handing it to Dick and Hill as of now. Like I should have done in the first place. What I want from you is five hundred words on how you know this fuckface. And I want it on my desk in half an hour. Tops.'

And then it hit me. Grace and Francisco had been in cahoots all along to concoct this whole preposterous scenario with the sole purpose of prompting my ignominious pratfall in the most spectacular fashion. There *was* no terrorist plot. There *was* no BBC programme scheduled. These were but malevolent lies devised to realise maximum professional discomfort. No sooner had this realisation struck me than it occurred to me that I no longer trusted myself to distinguish truth from lies. More than this; I no longer knew who I was. My past had been exposed as a lie and the remaining pages in the autobiography I'd been writing in my head were blank, having fallen into an abyss mid-sentence. I no longer recognised the self I'd always told myself I was. I'd become an imposter to myself. Retreating to the toilets to pull myself together, I glanced in the mirror and saw a stranger stare back at me.

I phoned Grace once more; not to give her the head's up this time, but to confirm or deny that I'd been the fall guy of an elaborate hoax. To determine my identity as either the gullible patsy or the heroic hack helping avert a major terrorist atrocity. My identity would rest on her response.

The phone rang. And rang. And rang until, just as I was about to replace the receiver, Grace answered abruptly and, disregarding the social etiquette of voicing a politely inquisitive 'Hello?', instead brusquely instructed me to meet her 'at The Space Bar in ten', hanging up before I'd even had a chance to identify myself – whoever I was – leaving me with little option but to obey her directive.

Ten minutes later, Grace rushed in looking harassed.

'Sorry – when you called I was on the receiving end of a tongue-lashing from my producer, demanding to know all the details of how I know Francisco, questioning my motives for the story, kicking me off the programme and handing all my work to a colleague – '

' – Snap,' I said, unable to disguise my relief that Grace's morning had been as tormented as my own, reassured that my fears she and Francisco had plotted to humiliate me were no more than the paranoid fantasies of the narcissistic self-delusionist I suspected myself to be.

'So … where do we stand?'

'In the dark,' she shrugged, beckoning the waitress and ordering a cappuccino from the hitherto carefree but suddenly sullen server who stopped humming a tune to herself the moment she recognised us. The cappuccino arrived and grew lukewarm before I tried again.

'So … how do we find our way back to the light?'

'We?'

'It feels like we're in this together. Whether we like it or not.'

'I'm not sure,' she said. 'But I'd say we'd best tread carefully. Very carefully.'

twelve

warped
reverie

I watched *Fake Flowers* on catch-up fully absorbed, having settled into my familiar indent on the well-worn once-white sofa with a bottle of *Grouse* within easy reach, having taken great care to settle Rose for the evening in advance, disconnecting the landline and switching off the mobile to enable immersion without interruption. My biased verdict was that it achieved a creditable job of presenting a convincing case that Francisco represented a serious terrorist threat to Tattoo spectators and anyone within the vicinity of Edinburgh castle.

Watching, I became aware of a rising tide of dread. A belated realisation that I'd waded too far from shore only to find myself adrift. Out of my depth. Caught in a current. The tide having turned. Marooning me. Leaving me stranded with everything that was once solid now diluted. Insubstantial. Fluid. Slipping through my fingers. Blurring my vision. Watering down my faith in certainty with doubt.

In the immediate silence into which I found myself plunged at the programme's culmination, my fevered thoughts conceived of a fleeting shameful fantasy wherein the media furore within which I'd become ensnared had escalated to a frenzied flux, having scaled a vertiginous crescendo climaxing in a spectacular deafening explosion at the Tattoo. Rather than stricken with grief for the multiple innocent victims and their families, my instinctive response was a warm, soothing infusion of satisfied relief that my warning, derided and unheeded, was validated and my rabid reactionary detractors reduced to chastising their own tawdry scepticism, kowtowing and proffering apologies as Kerr pled for me to return to my position where I was duly received back into the fold with a hero's welcome.

This warped reverie was interrupted by the unexpected

sustained high-pitched droning of my shrill doorbell, spiking my pulse with a potent injection of a toxic concoction of fear and self-loathing. I jumped to the conclusion that Francisco was standing on my doormat intent on physical or mental confrontation and retribution. An impatient knock at the door and the toxic concoction accelerated my mind in tandem with my rabbit heartbeat and I was stricken momentarily. Paralysed with fear. When the knocks grew louder, more frequent and more insistent, I realised that, unless I answered the door, Rose would be woken from her slumber with a cry of frustration and temper that would necessitate hours of devoted consolation to calm. I scanned the immediate vicinity, grabbed the *Grouse,* and approached the door warily, intent on clubbing the intruder over the head with the bottle if need be.

I yanked open the door with an exaggerated flourish of bravado in the hope of securing some advantage through an element of surprise, poised and armed for self-defence. Grace gave me a quizzical look. I pushed the door wider and stepped aside.

'I brought wine, but I see you're already hitting the hard stuff,' she said, nodding to the whisky I'd sought and failed to conceal.

Initially faltering and stilted, trickling, the conversation gradually began to flow more smoothly until it almost seemed like old times. We spoke about *Fake Flowers* and speculated what Francisco's next move might be. Then, apropos of nothing, Grace said,

'I want custody of Rose.'

Just like that. As flatly as if she were making small talk to fill in the gap of a dull conversation with a stranger at a bus stop. I had to ask her to repeat herself. She did so. It still struck me as incredulous.

'I'm back on my meds,' she added. 'Everything's under control. I'm capable of looking after her again. I promise. I need her. I need her in my life. She *is* my life. And I already told you: you're not her father.'

When it became evident that I was at a loss for words she said, 'Say something.'

'I don't believe you,' I said.

What I meant was that I didn't believe I was not Rose's father. In truth, I harboured doubts that I was. But I was not willing to concede the point without incontrovertible proof. What I did not mean was that I didn't believe that Grace was capable of looking after Rose. In truth, I harboured doubts that she was. But I had not intended to give voice to these doubts. That, though, was how Grace interpreted my statement. And that sparked an explosive loss of control.

A torrent of vindictive personal abuse, foul-mouthed threats of legal proceedings and ravings of imagined injustices spewed forth from her mouth in a raging torrent until, obeying the command of a sixth sense, Grace turned to find Rose standing, drowsily in her pyjamas in the doorway and stopped mid-rant. Rubbing her eyes and yawning, listening in, or perhaps sleepwalking, Rose's blank features were neither asleep nor quite awake. Grace had not set eyes on Rose since the night she'd abandoned us.

'Hello Rose,' she said. 'You're growing.'

Rose looked at her mum with unregistering eyes then turned and retreated into the shadows of the hallway, pushing her fringe back from her face. I leapt from the sofa to shepherd her safely back to slumberland. While I read her a chapter from her latest *Dr Seuss* before singing her favourite nursery rhyme over and over then feigning sleep with exaggerated snoring, I sought to process Grace's demand for custody. I was still doing so as I disentangled myself from Rose, climbed awkwardly from her soft squeaky mattress and returned to the living room to discover that Grace had vanished. Again.

thirteen

the disparity
between
fantasy
and reality

I texted Grace, requesting she let me know when she arrived home safely. She didn't respond. Nor did she bother to respond the following morning.

No sooner had I entered the newsroom that morning than I was beckoned by Kerr to join an editorial meeting with Dick and Hill to hear about the latest developments in their investigation into the ongoing terrorist threat. Before they could update us, the TV on the wall of Kerr's office reported the breaking news that the Prime Minister was to chair a Cobra meeting with senior ministers, security and intelligence officials and military chiefs at Whitehall that afternoon to co-ordinate and discuss the response of Her Majesty's Government to the threat.

Francisco, having been identified by the authorities as a person of interest, had reportedly 'gone to ground' and all ports, airports, train, and bus stations had been placed on high alert. My designated role at this meeting, Kerr explained to me with infinite impatience in a stilted, sceptical tone, as if attempting to instruct a recalcitrant toddler about the finer points of string theory, was to impart any useful insights into Francisco's character and background not already within the public domain that would set Dick and Hill off and running on a newsworthy line of enquiry unlikely to have been explored already by their competitors.

But as soon as it became apparent that I had no such insights, asides, anecdotes or perceptive reflections to divulge, my role was reduced rapidly to that of an eavesdropping by-stander whose continued presence could be justified only by the forlorn hope that some scrap of information pertinent to the story might pop impromptu into my head, at which point I'd be obliged to blurt it out if I was to have any hope of avoiding an abrupt dismissal to the newsroom to cover a piece on the sexual peccadilloes of the latest model in a never ending production line of prefab trans reality TV celebs.

A pause in the conversation.

'Anything you'd like to add?' asked Kerr. The mushrooming silence as I racked my brains for some scrap of information to utter was eventually interrupted, mercifully, by his phone ringing. He barked into it, glowered in my direction, and slammed down the handset.

'The police are here to see you,' he said. 'Report back as soon as they're done.'

～

DS Anderson and DC Whittaker were waiting for me in reception. It had been some time since their visit to question myself and Grace about the nature of our relationship with Francisco, but I recognised them immediately.

'Is Grace OK?' I asked

'Why?' asked Anderson, his tone reassuring me that his presence concerned a different matter entirely. I had jumped – erroneously I now realised – to the conclusion that the reason for their visitation had been to inform me, regretfully, that Grace's sudden disappearance and consequent lack of communication was due to the fact that she'd been abducted or identified as a victim of some horrendous accident or grievous bodily assault, or even suicide. I now scrambled to deflect my discomfiture by indicating my urgent need to determine if the meeting room was available and enquire if they cared for refreshments.

Once this ritual of social etiquette had been dispensed with and space to talk secured, Anderson explained the reason for his visit as Whittaker re-enacted his inability to make eye contact and his aptitude for scribbling diligently in his notepad.

'We're here about Francisco García,' he said. 'Any ideas where he might be?'

'None,' I answered. Truthfully. Anderson renewed his familiar strategy of letting the gaps in the conversation do the legwork. After a few seconds of this silent treatment, right on cue, I felt compelled to fill the void. 'If I knew where he was, believe me, I'd tell you. As I'm sure you're aware, you're not the only one looking for him,' I said, glancing over his shoulder towards Kerr's office. 'My editor for one is desperate to find him and expects me to know where he is too. But I don't.'

'When did you last see him?'

I explained that I'd interviewed Francisco a few days earlier about his play at the Fringe.

'D'you think he poses a genuine terrorist threat?'

'That's what I was about to ask you. You're the policeman. I'm only a journalist. Do *you*?'

Silence. 'Grace does,' I added, unable to resist filling in the blanks. 'And I don't think we can afford not to take the threat seriously.'

Anderson stroked his salt and pepper moustache, a new addition since our last encounter.

'What can you tell me about García that I don't already know?'

'How do *I* know what *you* do or don't know? All I know about him is in the piece I wrote in this morning's paper. All of which I suspect you knew already. But I suppose I can give you the dossier Grace prepared for the BBC doc, which I presume you've seen?'

'That'd be helpful,' he said. I fetched *Fake Flowers* from my desk drawer, returning to interrupt Anderson and Whittaker's conspiratorial whispers.

'You seemed perturbed about Grace earlier,' Anderson

commented, casting his line effortlessly while rifling through the dossier; it was, after all, a ritual he'd perfected through many years of daily practice.

'It's nothing. I was just awaiting a reply to a text.'

Silence.

'Is it unusual for her to fail to reply to a text?'

'Not particularly. We don't make a habit of texting.' I proceeded to fill the silence by adding the quite superfluous information that we were no longer together.

Anderson nodded.

'Where can I find her?'

'The BBC. Pacific Quay.'

As soon as they departed, I texted Grace to give her the head's up that the police were on their way, then returned to Kerr's office to reassure him that I'd no further developments to report.

'OK, here's the deal,' said Kerr. 'The Tattoo opens tonight; your press pass is on your desk. Dick and Hill will be there with a remit to snoop about to see if this García character deigns to show face while gathering some vox pops. Your brief is to write up a 750-word review of the opening ceremony. Got it?'

I nodded, knowing that any other response would be tantamount to demanding delivery of my P45 on the spot, even if it meant that I had to call upon my long-suffering mum to once again step into the baby-sitting breach at extremely short notice. I could only hope that she was not on one of her many last-minute Ryanair deals to Costa del Sol. Fortunately, she reminded me that she'd just recently returned from Marbella so would be delighted to babysit Rose.

It was tight, but I squeezed into my seat on Edinburgh Castle's esplanade between two spectators disgruntled greatly by my tardy approach to timekeeping interrupting their wine gum chewing and chocolate chomping just as the live link to the roar of a Spitfire gearing up for take-off from nearby Edinburgh Airport shook the air, precipitating an opening fanfare as the Massed Pipes and Drums marched through the castle gatehouse into the centre of the esplanade to a skirling traditional pipe band set. After an initial period of adjustment to the onslaught of this unabashed visual and aural assault, I was pleasantly surprised to find myself enraptured by the occasion; the dramatic setting; the unbridled revelry of my fellow spectators and the deafeningly bombastic pipe bands coming together to create a jarringly, tartan kitsch spectacle I'd not anticipated relishing. This was the start of an evening of pageantry, parade and performance which saw representation from what appeared to be every conceivable pipe band from the British Armed Forces and the farthest reaches of the Commonwealth, together with all possible manifestations of drill and display teams and Highland dancers and performers from across the globe.

As a haunting finale, The Massed Military Bands and Massed Pipes and Drums led an all-cast traditional ceilidh of *Strip the Willow* before segueing seamlessly into the *Evening Hymn, The Day Thou Gavest*, heralding the appearance of the Lone Piper, high on the castle ramparts, playing the lingering lament, *Crags of Tumbledown*. The poignant silence at the conclusion of this performance was shattered only by a deafening explosion of fireworks, precipitating a mass chorus of *Auld Lang Syne*, replete with no-holds-barred audience participation and the roar of the Spitfire swooping low and directly overhead.

I was thankful that the disparity between my shameful fantasy of the previous evening and reality meant that my reprehensible apparition of a media furore climaxing in a terrorist atrocity at the Tattoo had failed to materialise. The Tattoo's spectacular opening ceremony, rife with discrete heightened security measures, had passed without incident. At least on this occasion.

fourteen

same
difference

Tension heightened over the following days with myself in attendance at each succeeding Tattoo display like a nervy novice bombmaker attempting to assemble his first IED without a manual. The police and the National Counter Terrorism Security Office, together with considerable representation from Scotland's close-knit media community, had been hunting down Francisco for several days, but had still to unearth a solid line of enquiry. Rumours and hearsay were rife. Supposed fleeting sightings of Francisco were reported, investigated, and invariably found wanting. And Grace responded, eventually, to my texts, which struck me initially as a reversion to normality but, latterly, following several failed attempts to speak to her in person, started to niggle me, to the point where their unfamiliarity of tone and phraseology aroused in me a suspicion that she was not their author. But if not Grace, who? I arranged to meet with her to set my mind at rest.

Fresh from the usual palaver entailed in the deceptively simple task of depositing Rose at her gran's without being embroiled in a merciless quickfire interrogation of my lack of affairs, I sped to the address Grace had texted me in the west end. At least that was my destination. As I braked heavily at the pedestrian traffic lights on Gibson Street, an androgynous student sporting the textbook uniform de jour – shaved back and sides with floppy fringe, skip cap, cool specs, torn tee, shredded jeans and scuffed *Converse* with scruffy canvas rucksack strung over one shoulder – knocked on my passenger window and mouthed that they needed directions. I unwound the window. That was when they leapt into the passenger seat.

'Change of plan,' they said, in a voice that maintained their gender mystery. 'You're being followed. You're on your way to Grace, right? You're under surveillance. The authorities are waiting for you or Grace to lead them to your *friend*.'

'What the f– ?'

'I know. I know. But look, it's a flashing amber. I need you to turn left at the lights as if you're going to head up University Avenue. But, at the last minute, double back at the traffic island at the foot of the hill and come back along Bank Street. I'll give you directions from there. In the meantime – give me your phone. I need to prevent them from tracking you.'

They spoke with an authority that gave an assurance that they knew exactly what they were doing. I obeyed their instructions and, sure enough, the driver and passenger (two nondescript plain clothed thirtysomething males) of the car behind the car behind me were too taken aback by my sudden manoeuvre to disguise their surprise. My passenger delighted in giving them the finger as they sped past in the opposite direction.

'OK, make sure you get through these lights,' they instructed. I accelerated through an amber turning red. 'Keep the speed up,' they said, scrutinising the rear window. 'OK, second right.'

We took a sharp right then reversed down a cobbled lane alongside the Kelvin where my passenger jumped out, removed a couple of traffic cones safeguarding a lone parking space then guided me in. No sooner had I parked than they removed a cover from their rucksack, threw it over the car, and we ducked into a Sikh Temple.

We were led unhurriedly through to a room in the rear. My nameless guide returned my phone, instructed me to keep it switched off, stood aside for me to enter, then promptly shut the door behind me, standing guard on the outside. Inside the room, which rekindled sublimated memories of a school common room, though with dusty religious posters and paraphernalia adorning the phlegm-coloured walls, Grace sat on a grey plastic chair at an oval table beneath a large, imposing tromp l'oile depicting an unfamiliar biblical scene featuring disciples and soldiers and angels. The airless space held a lingering stale odour. The expression on her face, more accurately, the *lack* of expression on her face – she didn't seem in the least surprised to see me – robbed me of any fleeting sense of relief, alerting me instead to prepare myself for the ordeal to come.

Grace then pushed back her chair and led me down an airless hallway into a dim antechamber where Francisco was seated, cup of tea in one hand, interweaving around the fingers of the other a large transparent, yellow-handled Phillips screwdriver like a showboating heavy metal drummer twirling a drumstick. Although I had, inexplicably, anticipated Francisco's presence, his appearance unsettled me.

'Sandy!' Francisco greeted me enthusiastically, the charade of unfamiliarity deployed at our last encounter cast aside like an actor discarding a defunct masquerade.

Clad in black, with a gleam in his eye and a barely concealed smirk on his chiselled puss, Francisco looked every inch the international man of mystery playing cat and mouse on a high wire, but always keeping one step ahead of the two-left-footed authorities stumbling and fumbling around him like tutu wearing hippos in *Fantasia* while he pirouetted effortlessly, ducking and diving in and out and around and about them like Ali in his prime, revelling in the slap and tickle and tease and spectacle of his danse macabre. It was as if he'd adopted wholesale the composite persona of Henri Harrington/Lachlan Urquhart, the lead character he'd written for his thwarted Fringe production to resurrect it for this latest bravura performance.

Francisco's ersatz bonhomie was contrasted by Grace's subdued demeanour and wan pallor. I took a seat, warily, aware I'd stumbled into a minefield with no familiar landmarks to lend me a steer as to the ultimate destination of this unprecedented predicament. The only thing apparent was that Francisco was in his element. Grace and I were at his mercy, reduced, when confronted head on with the very real threat of imminent unvarnished visceral violence, to mute, pliable playthings for Francisco to manipulate at his whim.

'I understand you've been looking for me,' he teased.

'I take it you were the author of the texts that were purportedly from Grace?'

Francisco confirmed this with the re-emergence of the smirk I vowed to wipe from his smug mug at the earliest opportunity.

'For what purpose?'

'To reunite the three of us.'

'For what purpose?'

'To decide what happens next.'

'What happens next?'

'That depends on you.'

'How so?'

His answer was another smirk. I looked to Grace for guidance. Her attention was fixed on a knot in the wood of the creaking floorboards.

'On whether you – both of you – decide to co-operate. Or not,' he said. I shrugged and waited for him to proceed. 'Both of you're under pressure, from employers and the authorities, to provide some useful insight about me to help them understand my motive and track me down. Correct?'

Despite some reluctance, myself and Grace confirmed this to be the case.

'Good. Well let's give them what they want!' Francisco hollered theatrically. 'And please accept my gratitude for *Fake Flowers*,' he added. 'Fortunately, or unfortunately, depending on where you're standing, it simultaneously got entirely the wrong end of the stick *and* conveyed *exactly* the message I hoped it might...'

'How so?' asked Grace.

'Because, rather than an executor of atrocities, as you claimed erroneously, The Amino's comprised of fake actors hired, in this instance, to reveal the failings in our client's security measures. Rather than a plot to commit a terrorist atrocity resulting in multiple fatalities, *Fake Flowers* is nothing other than a covert simulation exercise conceived to test the robustness of The Tattoo in this age of radical terrorism within which we now find ourselves. It was conceived to expose any deficiencies in security to demonstrate how it can be safeguarded effectively *against* terrorist attack! Apologies if that reality's too mundane and less news-worthy than the urgent impending catastrophe warning *fantasy* headline you craved. But what you reported – both of you – was *exactly* what we wanted you to.'

'Who's your client?' asked Grace.

'Our client has no wishes to waive his rights to anonymity at this particular juncture,' he answered.

'So how can we verify the veracity of your claim that this is nothing but a simulation exercise?' I asked.

'You can't,' he smiled. 'That's the *point*! But you *do* have my word that there will be *precisely zero* fatalities as a direct consequence of our activities.'

'What are words worth?' asked Grace, rhetorically.

'Not as much as action. Or *inaction*,' said Francisco.

'Meaning?'

'Meaning, the fact that I've thus far refrained from ramming this screwdriver into your eye socket must mean *something*!' he erupted, before asking, in a more conciliatory tone, 'surely you can see that my... restraint... would be irrational if my intention was to carry out a terrorist atrocity? Surely I'd have rid myself of you both by now to stop you foiling my reprehensible plan by informing the authorities?' he posited, carving a question mark in the air with his screwdriver as he did so, before pointing it lazily at each of us in turn.

'But what about your obituary, the footage of you at Girona Airport and all the other stuff Grace unearthed about you and The Amino?' I asked.

'Well, I needed a back story, didn't I?' he winked.

'So,' said Grace, 'now that you've told us that the supposed terrorist plot is nothing other than a drill designed to uncover any security loopholes, I presume you wish us to report just that?'

'Exactly.'

'But would that not nullify the simulation, by exposing it as such?'

'*Not* exactly.'

'Why not?' asked Grace, frowning.

'Because the authorities can't afford to accept his claim that it's nothing other than a simulation exercise at face value. They'll need to proceed to treat the threat as genuine, whether or not it transpires to be fake,' I interjected. 'It's the same difference, whether or not the threat's real.'

'*Exactly!*' exclaimed Francisco.

⁓

'What's our next move?' asked Grace when we were deposited outside, blinking in the daylight.

'We report back on Francisco's claim that the threat's fake and nothing more menacing than a simulation exercise,' I said.

'You think we should accept what he told us at face value?'

'Not at all. I think we should report what he said but retain a sceptical stance and suggest that we can't afford to accept his claims at face value. And I don't think we should leave anything out.'

'Such as?'

'I think we should mention the fact that he refused to divulge the identity of his client. I know that Kerr – and I'm sure your producer – will be keen to get some investigative guys on the case to uncover whose paying for this *simulation exercise*. I suppose the starting point would be to quiz the organisers of The Tattoo about whether or not *they* commissioned it.'

'They're hardly going to admit as much if they *did*, are they? And if such an exercise did exist, it's likely that only a ridiculously small coterie would be party to its existence. Otherwise the whole exercise would be rendered redundant.'

'No,' I admitted. 'But at least it's a start. We have to be seen to ask the question.'

In the event, neither of us were taken aback when our enquiries hit a dead end. Neither The Royal Edinburgh Military Tattoo nor the National Counter Terrorism Security Office claimed any knowledge of the existence of a simulation exercise codenamed *Fake Flowers*.

fifteen

killer
heels

Despite the urgent need to determine whether the planned terrorist attack on the Tattoo did or did not represent a genuine threat to hundreds if not thousands of lives, I found myself distracted by the Post Office's lax approach to the schedule of its 'guaranteed' delivery service. Matters of a personal nature, it seems, outweigh those of the public. I'd been tracking the delivery of my package for several days now and the estimated time and date of arrival had altered on a couple of occasions already so there was a degree of uncertainty over when I could expect the results.

Aside from frustration at the ever-shifting delivery dates, I seemed incapable of anticipating what my reaction would or should be to the results whenever they did finally arrive. While I expected the paternity test to confirm my suspicion that Francisco was Rose's biological father, what if the results proved inconclusive? But if they showed that Francisco *was* Rose's biological father, then on what grounds could I deny Grace's plea for custody of Rose? And if I didn't know how I'd react to the result then might it not be for the best that I didn't know it? Would my relationship with Rose differ if I discovered that Francisco was her father? If so, how? Would my relationship differ if I discovered that Francisco was *not* her father? If so, how? I'd like to think that the result would have zero effect on our relationship. Why, then, had I ordered the paternity test? What good could come of it? And yet I needed to know. It had something to do with a need to know the truth. Whatever *that* is. Once I knew the truth, I told myself, then, somehow, I'd just know how to respond, how to feel and what measures, if any, to take.

Having reported the details of our encounter with Francisco and my claims about the alleged terrorist plot to Kerr, I was dispatched to return to the Sikh Temple accompanied by Dick and Hill on babysitting duty, between whom I was sandwiched like a riding bitch in the back of a fast black. They quizzed me incessantly en route, transcribing each of my stumbling mumblings into indecipherable shorthand hieroglyphics in wire bound notepads. Stuck there between Dick and Hill, I was stabbed by the pangs of the inexplicable guilt of the incompetent innocent suspect.

It transpired that the temple was locked and, apparently, empty. That didn't curtail the dynamic duo from taking it in turns to pummel the door with their fists and kick it with their heels to no avail, while making calls to various contacts who furnished them with a number for the temple and the name of its leader. Dick then dialled the number and the three of us listened to the phone ring out inside the locked building. We hung around until our resignation outweighed our all-too predictable expletive-filled frustration then repeated the black cab journey in reverse. Throughout, I was subjected to an intensified interrogation about my meeting with Francisco interrupted intermittently by calls to their trusted contacts at The Tattoo and NaCTSO to determine whether there was any truth in Francisco's claim that this was nothing other than a drill aimed at testing procedures in preparation for a terrorist attack. Their calls were met with definitive denials. As far as the authorities were concerned, the threat was genuine.

Back at base we debriefed Kerr whose spontaneous eruption of a volcano of expletives made Dick and Hill seem like twin pillar fatalistic zen masters of serenity. Kerr barked orders at me to draft up a piece on my version of events and at Dick and Hill to persevere with their attempts to contact the leader of the temple to uncover the nature of its connection with a terrorist suspect – under strict instructions to proceed with caution, not to jump to any conclusions, make any assumptions or cast any aspersions about linking the terrorist threat to the local Sikh community.

"And, above all, *all three of you*, I want you to uncover the identity of this psycho's mystery client!" he thundered.

Just how we were expected to do that was beyond me. Though Dick and Hill knew Glasgow's underworld intimately, and knew people who knew people in subterranean Edinburgh, I suspected that the higher echelons of international terrorist networks resided somewhere in a galaxy far beyond their ken too. It was fortunate, then, that, just as we'd resigned ourselves to contemplation of our messy confrontation at high speed with a dead end in our inept attempts to uncover the identity of Francisco's client, events should intervene to swipe the dead end away and lead us instead on a magical mystery tour of our own devising, destination unknown. No sooner had we departed his company than our agitated editor summoned us back into his office to inform us that our presence had been *requested* (it had been made clear that non-attendance was not an option) at an urgent meeting with the security services at BBC Scotland's HQ.

A brisk taxi ride over the Clyde and we were met outside the landmark reflective box that is home to BBC Scotland. From there we were fast-tracked through the security procedures and led to a smart if impersonal conference room affording an impressive panorama over the river and the cityscape beyond.

Not that we had much time to contemplate the vista as no sooner had polite but guarded introductions been made with our BBC hosts (Grace, her producer and head of news) who, it was apparent, had been impatiently awaiting our arrival, than we were joined by the meeting's convener.

I heard the click clack of her killer heels before I saw her – and I just knew that they had to be glossy pillar box red. For once, the reality didn't fall short of the fantasy. If anything, it transcended it. Her hip-swaying catwalk strut, choreographed tap dance steps across the tiled floored open plan office, sounded like the finger-popping intro to some mid 50s Sonny Rollins track signifying the fizzing hum electrical static entrance of a femme fatale firing off sparks come to shake things up and skew things onto a quite different, danger-laden course to what might have been expected to transpire otherwise. Kerr, moments before a fevered portrait of a tightly wound ball of barely stifled frustration framed by the doorway making small talk with his BBC counterpart, stepped aside, and signalled for her to enter with a curt bow like a bellhop hopeful of a generous tip. If he'd been wearing a hat he'd have doffed it. Together with his counterpart, he followed her into the conference room.

'Gentlemen… *and* **lady,**' noted the killer-heeled convenor with a nod of sisterly solidarity to Grace. 'Thanks for gathering at such short notice. I'm Agent Lee. This meeting is off-record,' she addressed Kerr and his BBC counterpart, a statement of fact that invited no protest.

'Of course,' they duly acquiesced in unison.

Turning her attention to Dick and Hill, she said, 'So you won't be needing these,' indicating their poised pens. After glancing towards Kerr, the hard-boiled hacks huffed and puffed in stereo, threw down their pens in a temper tantrum, folded their arms like naughty schoolboys and frowned their displeasure.

'Thank you for your co-operation,' said Lee. 'Much appreciated. Let's begin. I work with MI6.' Here she fished a Secret Intelligence Service ID card from a pocket and flashed it at the room. 'My colleague Agent Gray has some classified information he'd like to share with you,' she said, turning to encourage her hitherto invisible assistant seated to her left to open his attaché case and distribute its contents around the table. 'But first, the Non-Disclosure Agreements.'

Gray was a bald bespectacled overweight fifty-something nondescript civil servant-type wearing an ill-fitting crumpled grey suit with an impeccably knotted striped old school tie (the same tie, I noticed, sported by the BBC Head of News whose name I didn't quite catch) and threadbare brown suede *Hush Puppies* evidently chosen for comfort over style. If he was a spook, and it appeared that he was, however junior his rank and administrative his function, he killed any James Bond fantasies of glamour stone dead at first glance. Once he'd inspected our signatures on the legal documents to his satisfaction, Gray distributed a second set of papers.

'I can't stress highly enough the classified nature of these documents,' Lee emphasised. 'This concerns a matter of utmost import to national security. The sole purpose of this meeting is to reveal to you the contents of this confidential account in order to convince you that there's absolutely no truth in the claim made by the terrorist suspect earlier today to your reporters Ms Robertson and Mr Young – ' here she nodded to Grace and myself in turn ' – that he'd been instructed, by us or anyone else, to conduct a simulation exercise to test the robustness of security at the Edinburgh Tattoo. No truth whatsoever.'

As she spoke, the attendees flicked through the files, attempting to digest the dense legalese acronym-heavy paragraph-length spook-speak sentences, each laden with detailed minutiae and material in parenthesis and numerous asterisks and bullet-pointed subclauses, not to mention abbreviated footnotes and heavily redacted sections. As they did so, they nodded their heads, pretending that they got the gist.

'Let me be clear: this was no simulation exercise,' Lee reiterated. 'Rather, as you can see from these extensive files, we, in tandem with our European counterparts, have been tracking this suspect and his associates across the continent for some time and, having accumulated a considerable volume of intelligence, arrived at the conclusion that he represents a genuine security threat. Ideally, we'd have apprehended the suspect in Edinburgh, as planned, without anyone being any the wiser – as is the norm. Instead, thanks to your hastily compiled reports and *insight* into the suspect's background, we find ourselves in the unfortunate position of mass panic at the prospect of a terrorist threat. Fortunately, that panic can now be significantly assuaged.'

'How so?' interjected the BBC head of news.

'Because the suspect was apprehended a little over an hour ago and is now safely in custody. Members of the public can take some assurance from the fact that the threat of a terrorist incident at The Tattoo has been downgraded from critical to moderate. In fact, your First Minister and the Prime Minister will be making co-ordinated statements to that effect, and announcing the disbandment of the Cobra committee, on the steps at Bute House and Downing Street within the hour.'

'Where and how did you capture the suspect?' demanded Dick, with his customary casual disrespect.

'That information's classified,' replied Lee, unflustered.

'Where's he being held?' demanded Hill.

'Ditto,' deadpanned Lee.

After a brief pause, Kerr felt obliged to contribute on behalf of his profession before his peers and colleagues. He cleared his throat uncomfortably.

'Firstly, thanks for the heads-up about the impending ministerial statements,' he began, revealing a hitherto hidden aptitude for diplomacy. 'As I'm sure you'd agree, freedom of the press lies at the heart of our democratic conventions and unwritten constitution. As such, as members of the press, it's our obligation to probe, question and subject to scrutiny the authorities in order to ascertain the truth about these events for the general public, which is why my colleagues are only trying to do their jobs by finding out some simple essential facts to enable them to report on the latest developments – '

' – let me assure you,' interrupted Lee, 'that I'm intimately familiar with, and fully supportive of, the important role played by the press and the need to respect its freedoms. As such, in due course, I hope to be as informative as I can. I'd hope too that the media will acknowledge that, since a threat, albeit moderate, of terrorist activity remains, there's an urgent need for the security services to retain confidentiality over certain sensitive items of information until such time as it's determined that a terrorist threat has been nullified, given that it's removing the threat to civilians that remains our primary priority.'

'But the public's got a right to know the facts!' interjected

Dick.

Lee sighed, but before she could muster the will to reiterate her point, Agent Gray intervened on her behalf to reveal that he had never been anywhere near the service of the diplomatic corps.

'Listen,' he hissed, with barely concealed disdain, 'We're combating terrorist threats everyday while you're down the boozer or lying in your bed nursing your hangover or scribbling your sensationalist exclusives on the latest kneecappings, stabbings and shootings between local criminal gangs over their inane little drug turf wars. If you're so concerned about facts, perhaps it'd be an idea to contact us prior to ploughing ahead with broadcasting and publishing ill-informed stories rife with inaccuracies, pet theories and sensationalism designed to incite mass panic without pause for thought of the consequences for the public?'

His statement ended in a rising intonation that suggested a question mark, but those on the receiving end of it were left in no doubt that, if this was indeed a question, it was rhetorical.

There followed a sometimes heated sometimes lacklustre ping-pong debate about press freedom and responsibility, government propaganda, black propaganda, misinformation, disinformation, false balance, bothsideism, fabrication and fake news, none of which was remotely enlightening or constructive or shifted either side from its entrenched position. When she could bear it no longer, Lee brought the meeting to a conclusion by rising to her feet, thanking everyone for their attendance at such short notice and exiting with Gray in tow.

Before departing I glanced over at Grace, who, distracted, wore a discomfited expression like a miscast bit-part actor out of her depth who'd forgotten her lines underneath the spotlight and wished that a trapdoor would open to facilitate her swift exit from the stage. The fact that we'd had no opportunity to exchange confidences in private irritated me for the remainder of the afternoon. It was a feeling that grew with each successive unanswered text.

sixteen

que
sera
sera

An hour later, just as Agent Lee had said they would, Scotland's First Minister and Britain's Prime Minister made carefully crafted and coordinated reassuring pronouncements about the 'successful operation conducted by the security forces acting swiftly and decisively on intelligence which had resulted in the capture of a terrorist suspect' and the subsequent downgrading of the widely reported terrorist threat at the Tattoo. While neither politician took more than a couple of questions from reporters, the fact that the operation referred to remained ongoing suggested that intelligence forces were actively on the hunt for other members of the terrorist cell. While Kerr had dispatched political and Westminster correspondents to cover the politicians' statements, Dick and Hill were assigned to uncover as much detail as they could about Francisco's arrest. I was instructed to write up a piece on my encounter with Francisco and his claim that the alleged terrorist plot was no more than a simulation exercise.

That evening, while I tried and failed to catch the news while getting Rose ready for bed, she blurted out 'Mummy!', pointing at the screen. Following her line of vision, I saw Grace in the newsroom being quizzed by the anchor about our meeting with Francisco that morning and her account of his subsequent arrest. Turning up the volume, I listened as Grace answered her colleagues' gentle pre-scripted questioning with carefully considered responses that echoed the ministerial pronouncements that the terrorist threat had, to all intents and purposes, been quashed and that the authorities were confident that the Tattoo and the wider Edinburgh Festival would continue without incident, though heightened security measures would remain in place as a precaution.

An hour later, with Rose sound, the doorbell rang.

'Can I come in? I want to see Rose.'

I retreated to the kitchen as Grace popped into Rose's bedroom alone to steal a precious minute or so to torture herself with a glimpse of her sleeping daughter, falling slow motion into mute wonder at the delicacy of her features, inhaling hungrily her infant scent, reflecting on her pregnancy from conception to delivery, the hopes and sunny anticipation at the miracle of creation and the sky-high aspirations to the inexplicable hollow dark and darkening emptiness enveloping her world in a mushroom cloud shroud into which she'd stumbled unwittingly in its aftermath. At least that's what I imagine went through her head.

Returning to the living room, Grace lost in silent contemplation, her mind wandered somewhere far away and long ago while I watched from the couch patiently, quietly, waiting for her to return to the present tense in her own time. When she did so, it was to declare, 'I'm lost. I feel dizzy. I've lost track of what's real and what's... not. I think I've been floundering for some time now. I'm not sure what or who to believe anymore. Or who to trust.'

After what I considered to be a decent interval, when it seemed she'd stalled, I said, 'You can trust me.'

Grace looked at me anew, scrutinizing my features as though searching for a fragment of recognition.

'And why should I trust *you*?' she asked. 'After... everything?'

Again, I didn't rush to reply, but when I did, it was to suggest, gently, '*Because* of everything.'

After a while, Grace disturbed the settled, secure quiet by

tossing a live grenade into my unsuspecting lap.

'What would you do in the event of a three-minute warning?' she asked. When I responded with an expression of perplexity, she added, 'Don't tell me you've never thought about it.'

'I haven't.'

'*Everybody's* thought about it.'

'*I* haven't.'

'Yes, you have.'

'Well, if the siren was to sound right now, I'd firstly tiptoe through to the bedroom and kiss Rose tenderly on the forehead, wish her sweet dreams, then close her door gently behind me, open another bottle, take you in my arms, if you'd let me, and confess that it's only ever been you that's made my life worth living. That I've always loved you. That I love you still. That I'll love you for all eternity. In this life and the next.'

When Grace failed to offer up a response, I eventually felt compelled to prompt her. 'And you?'

She released a long sigh before deigning to answer.

'Que sera sera,' she said.

~ ⌇ ~

The following morning I spied a jiffy bag stuffed into the letterbox. I knew immediately what it was. I tore the package open to discover, finally, the result of the paternity test. I interrupted my cursory scan of the introductory text to jump straight down to the result, before retracing my steps and re-reading the short introductory information repeatedly, each time more slowly. I'd understood the result but seemed to be searching for something more. It took me some time to concede what the something more I was searching for was. I was searching for some clue about how I should react to the result.

The result of the paternity test was that there was a 96.7 per cent probability that Francisco was not Rose's father. I felt robbed of a sense of quiet satisfaction by a sense of bewilderment. Having convinced myself that Francisco was Rose's father, now that the paternity test had proved otherwise, I was at a loss about how now to see Francisco. How to see Grace. How to see myself. And how to see Rose. Even though, I told myself, I'd already decided that I'd view Rose no differently. And this was indeed how I felt. Even if the same could not be said with conviction about how I felt about Francisco. Or Grace. Or myself.

And then an obvious path to clarification struck me and I cursed my stupidity for not having thought of it before. Why hadn't I applied the paternity test to myself? Could Grace be mistaken in thinking I was not Rose's father? Or might she have sought deliberately with malice aforethought to inflict some cruel vindictive suffering by feeding me the lie that I wasn't Rose's father? I vowed to order another test and take it as soon as practicably possible, cursing myself once more for not having thought of doing so earlier.

seventeen

this
is
for
real

The eventful day that was set to unfold was characterised initially by a dead weight settling deep within the heart of Francisco's core. A subliminal sense of humdrum mundanity and constraint having taken root to spread a diseased weakening hollowing out health and vitality. While not physically shackled, he was defeated utterly. Closed and resigned to his fate. Having stumbled into a cul-de-sac, he raised his vision to find he'd somehow wound up at the terminal endgame. Reflective as a mirror and as devoid of depth, he was mesmerised dumbly by the dull glow lure of the eternal void lurking just beneath the surface. Every lethargic thought meant moving a mountain of effort such that he derived crumbs of comfort from his constraint. Lack of freedom provided respite from the need to decide for himself what or what not to do now.

At 11:00 hours a convoy of motorbikes, cars and an armour-plated van containing counter terrorism police set off from the heavily fortified Scottish Terrorist Detention Centre in Govan to transport him the short journey to Glasgow High Court where he appeared in private to face charges under Section 5 of the Terrorism Act 2000, concerning the facilitation, planning, organisation and conspiracy to commit acts of terrorism. The accused made no plea or declaration, was remanded in custody by Sheriff John Muir and given a date to appear the following week for full committal. Within minutes the convoy began its return journey to Govan. Francisco's appearance in court had taken no longer than five minutes. His return to his cell in Govan should have taken no more than ten. In the event, the return journey was never completed.

Francisco's morning might have begun with the feather descent of a numbing ennui, but his court appearance transpired to be only the prelude to an interlude of violence resulting in a scandalous escape from justice as a terrorist gang disguised as rescue services personnel, hi-jacked the convoy with ambulances and a fire engine to snatch freedom for the accused from the clutches of captivity, leaving behind the mutilated corpses of five men and two women to litter the street like roadkill.

While the exact circumstances of how this shocking incident unfolded remains unclear, various eyewitness accounts reported a deafening blast followed quickly by a series of other explosions punctuated by intermittent bursts of rapid machine gun fire. A number of shaky and blurred footage from mobile phones held at tenement windows on either side of the street served to corroborate these reports. They showed a pair of blue-lit ambulances, sirens blaring, approaching the convoy at speed on either side from the rear, separating it, intercepting it and swerving deliberately to knock policemen from motorbikes. Simultaneously, a fire engine roared from a side street to ram the armour-plated van carrying Francisco with a sickening smash, sending it spinning out of control with a screech of wheels, collapsing on its side and skidding across the road, coming to rest a steaming, leaking heap of shattered glass and mangled metal.

Three of four firemen in full uniform with helmet and breathing apparatus in place, armed with heavy axes and wire cutters alongside what were later identified as AK47 machine guns, leapt from the fire engine and calmly, methodically, set about freeing Francisco from the wrecked van, moments before it erupted into a flaming inferno with three policemen trapped inside.

Francisco was bundled into one of the two ambulances, which, together with the fire engine, rushed from the scene, the traffic parting obediently before them to ease their escape. The convoy appeared to be transporting Francisco straight back to Govan, from where a police helicopter took off from Glasgow City Heliport to monitor its route and help co-ordinate the chase, before diverting into the Clyde tunnel, ducking out of site of the helicopter, which hovered above the tunnel's exit, waiting for the convoy's re-emergence. It was not until a convoy of police cars entered the tunnel to discover the fire engine and ambulances abandoned at its mid-way point that it became apparent that Francisco and his gang had switched to a getaway car lying in wait to make good their escape.

When the smouldering burnt out shell of a silver *Vauxhall Corsa* was discovered abandoned on the edge of an industrial estate on the outskirts of Drumchapel some hours later, the police were able to match its registration plate to that of a silver *Vauxhall Corsa* seen emerging from the Clyde tunnel less than a minute after the convoy of fire engine and ambulances had entered it. Within the hour Dick revealed that he'd been informed by an anonymous, though reliable, source that a rose gold fabric flower had been left displayed on the dashboard of the abandoned fire engine.

One thing was now certain: there was no longer any doubt about whether the terrorist threat to the Edinburgh Military Tattoo was genuine or a simulation exercise. The corpses of five men and two women in the mortuary put paid to that debate. This was for real.

eighteen

execution
speculation

Riddled with guilt, steeped in shame, a mute observer, rendered obsolete, terrorised, I stalled, watching myself watching footage of Francisco's blood-soaked escape unfold. As the live news bulletin reported that the threat of a terrorist incident at The Tattoo had been upgraded from moderate to critical and that the Prime Minister had reconvened an emergency meeting of the Cobra committee, my guilt spiked. Even if I were at a loss to identify what I could or should have done differently. Both the British Prime Minister and Scotland's First Minister issued brief statements expressing their condolences to the families of the yet to be named police officers who lost their lives in the line of duty and stressed that their top priority was to hunt down and capture the perpetrators of that morning's murderous attack on justice. It was left to the news anchor in the studio and her colleague at the scene of the carnage to exchange speculations about whether the murderous atrocity would lead to the cancellation of that evening's finale to the Tattoo.

The first call I made was to my mum to arrange for her to pick up and look after Rose. The second was to Grace to check she was up to speed with the latest developments, for which solicitude I received a distracted single word confirmation before the line went dead. The third was set to be to DS Anderson to inform him of my encounter with Francisco and subsequent appointment with Agents Lee and Gray at the BBC but, distracted mid-dial by a sixth sense, I turned to see Anderson, accompanied as ever by Whittaker, approach my desk.

The policemen led me to their car and sped to the Sikh Temple only to find it smouldering, cordoned off and in the process of being inspected forensically by a trio of white disposable-suited and booted crime scene investigators immersed fully in the methodical task of taking swabs and extracting samples for analysis. The head of this unit broke briefly from overseeing this meticulous scientific search for evidence to inform Anderson that the temple had been the subject of a suspicious arson attack during the night, but that there were no immediately obvious signs of evidence at the scene, which suggested a professional job, but he would prioritise the identification of any evidence gathered and revert asap.

From there, I was whisked to Govan Street station to be reunited with Grace and Agents Lee and Gray, both of whose disposition differed markedly from that of the previous day. Their air of authoritative control had been replaced by barely contained unease.

'If you had to guess – ' started Gray.

' – and you *do*,' interjected Lee.

' – where do you think Francisco García is *right now*?' finished Gray.

'I've no idea why you should think that *we* should have any idea,' I said, answering for myself and Grace.

'Because you and Ms Robertson were the last people known to have met him prior to his arrest,' said Lee.

'Well, I can assure you that he didn't tell us anything about his plans to execute a terrorist atrocity,' I said. 'But if you're demanding to know where I think he's most likely to be at this very minute – '

' – and I *am*,' interjected Lee.

' – I'd say that he's either en route to, or already at, Edinburgh Castle with the aim of executing said terrorist atrocity.'

'And if *you* had to guess – ' started Gray, addressing Grace.

' – and you *do*,' interjected Lee.

' – what kind of attack do you think he has planned?' finished Gray.

'If I had to guess – and yeah, I know, I know, *I do*, ' said Grace, with barely concealed contempt, 'I'd think any planned terrorist attack is likely to be a grand gesture and that, rather than a small-scale solo mission, it will involve a number of people to pull off. And be spectacular. With the prospect of maximising civilian casualties. Which is why I think you should cancel the Tattoo.'

'Cancellation isn't an option,' said Lee, rising and smoothing an imaginary crease from her blouse. 'You're coming with us,' she said to Grace and myself.

'Where are we going?' asked Grace.

'Edinburgh Castle,' said Lee.

nineteen

sub
plot

A drive east along the M8 in a blacked out armour-plated *Land Rover* sandwiched between a convoy of blue-lit police cars travelling at a speed well above the national limit passed mostly in interminable silence. When the silence began to fester and weep and itch like an infected wound, Lee instructed the driver to turn on the radio to provide a distraction from the suffocating conversational vacuum. The car's occupants listened distractedly to a round table discussion comprising a panel of terrorism and defence experts offering their informed analyses on the ramifications of that morning's fatal incident and the likely nature of the consequent manhunt. The heated discussion, which gave vent to a variety of contradictory heartfelt advice and opinion based on competing research, compelling evidence, prejudice and politics, culminated in the airing of a police statement encouraging the public to be its 'eyes and ears' by reporting potentially crucial information about any suspicious activity confidentially on 0800 78932 or, in the event of an emergency, 999.

When the live discussion was followed by a news roundup, a bulletin sparked Grace to blurt out a half-formed question as much as for herself as for her fellow passengers to attempt to answer. Following the lead item on Francisco's blood-soaked escape and its aftermath, the next concerned a parade scheduled for that evening at Her Majesty's Naval Base Clyde to mark half a century since the Ministry of Defence began its nuclear deterrent patrols by submarines armed with nuclear weapons. The item included a comment from the Secretary of State for Defence, scheduled to deliver a keynote speech at the event, which was to be attended by a slew of political, defence, military personnel and other worthies and dignitaries.

He said that the 'golden anniversary of the continuous-at-sea deterrent, Operation Relentless, the longest ever carried out by the UK's armed forces, at Faslane naval base on Gare Loch, would be a special memorial commemoration recognising the commitment of our submariners and the success of the continuous-at-sea deterrent provided by a quartet of Vanguard-class submarines carrying Trident missiles'.

'What if there's a sub plot?' Grace wondered aloud.

'A what?' asked Lee.

'A sub plot.'

'Explain,' ordered Gray.

'What if the Tattoo's just the distraction that has us all looking east... when the real threat's... in the west?' speculated Grace.

'Faslane,' I said, catching up with her train of thought.

'Did García ever mention nuclear weapons to either of you?' pressed Lee. When both Grace and I failed to respond, she added the coda, 'Think. Carefully.'

After a pause, I declared with solemn conviction, 'No.'

After another pause, all eyes fell on Grace who declared, with matching solemnity and conviction, a contradictory affirmation.

'So, which is it?' demanded Gray, impatiently.

'It's yes,' said Grace. 'The summer we met Francisco in L'Estartit, we discovered that, like us, he was a Dalí aficionado. He effectively acted as our tour guide around the Dalí Triangle – '

' – and?' interrupted Gray.

'Well, it was en route to The Dalí Theatre Museum in Figueres from Portlligat that he touched on Dalí's Mystical Manifesto.'

'His what?' asked Gray.

'Mystical Manifesto,' I interjected. 'I'd forgotten about that.

The atomic explosion at Hiroshima in 1945 *terrified* Dalí. But that terror gave birth to his theory of nuclear mysticism.'

'His what?' asked Gray.

'Nuclear mysticism. At its core it's what one gallery described as being what Dalí saw as *'an affinity between the invisible workings of the mind and the invisible mechanisms of subatomic particles'*. I remember Francisco telling us about how Hiroshima led Dalí on a quest to understand the hidden powers and laws of things in order to control them. And he mentioned that Dalí had written somewhere about having an extraordinary weapon available to him – '

' – What kind of weapon?' interrupted Gray.

'Mysticism,' answered Lee, choosing that moment to reveal her own knowledge of Dalí. 'Or what he referred to as *'the deep intuition of an immediate communion with the whole, absolute vision through the grace of truth, by divine grace."*

'What's any of this got to do with Faslane?' asked Gray.

'I mentioned it only to confirm that Francisco *did* mention nuclear weapons to us,' said Grace, defensively. 'If it's relevant or if there's any connection to Faslane, then it's beyond me.'

'*Everything's* connected,' insisted Lee, 'but finding the connection's beyond most people.' Her mobile already at her ear, she proceeded to issue curt instructions for a tactical unit to race to Faslane as a matter of urgency. Simultaneously, Gray instructed a contact already on the ground at Faslane to be on high alert for suspicious activity as a consequence of a real and present terrorist attack, the precise nature of which remained unclear, but which they believed was planned to coincide with that evening's ceremony.

'Is it beyond you?' I asked Lee.

'Well, I guess we'll soon find out. One way or another.'

'What about us? Should we do a U-turn and head east?' asked Grace.

'No,' said Lee. 'There may well be a sub plot, as you suggest… but whether the threat's east or west we're not at present in a position to say. So, we'll continue as planned.'

I searched Grace's face for a sign to help me read her thoughts. Her expression remained inscrutable.

'How many times have you two been asked to tell us about your relationship with García?' asked Lee, rhetorically. 'And yet you're only telling us about his interest in nuclear weapons now? Anything else you'd like to divulge?'

Grace and I were a picture of contrition.

'Who're you texting?' demanded Gray of Grace.

'My head of news,' replied Grace, guiltily. 'To tell him to get someone over to Faslane.'

'I'd better advise mine too,' I said. As I texted Kerr, on impulse I decided to copy in DS Anderson.

Lee then instructed Gray to ascertain the timings of the memorial commemoration at Faslane and The Tattoo, learning that the former was scheduled for a 5.30pm start and planned to last for an hour, while the latter was scheduled to start at 8.30pm and last until 10pm. Consulting her watch and calculating the time it would take to get to Faslane, she then reversed her decision and instructed the driver to undertake a U-turn and head to Faslane at top speed.

twenty

life
in the
faslane

It was the sinister synergy of Freedom of Information and Google that had sparked Francisco's embryonic plot. Readily available reports from the UK government's nuclear safety watchdog criticising the Ministry of Defence highlighted a high risk of a growing shortage of suitably qualified and experienced nuclear engineers at Faslane and quoted expert commentators' views that this lack of skilled staff represented 'the principal threat to the delivery of nuclear safety'. And so he'd scouted and sourced and groomed and welcomed a smart young nuclear engineer with idealistic, albeit dubious, politics, unquestioning loyalties, and non-existent ethics into The Amino. And, by following the laws of supply and demand, he was soon able, through the deployment of various double agents embedded at different levels within several UK government departments, to secure his young nuclear scientist a position at Faslane some months previously.

Simultaneously, when an online search turned up a report of £2.1 million worth of damage to the £1billion submarine *HMS Ambush* following a collision with the tanker *MV Andreas* off the coast of Gibraltar while on a training exercise after leaving its home port of Faslane, Francisco scouted and sourced and groomed and welcomed a fully qualified chief mate with extensive experience on various merchant vessels into The Amino. And he managed to secure him a position on Stena Line's *Superfast VII* operating between Belfast and Cairnryan, the route of which, he calculated, would take it within reasonable proximity to submarines entering and leaving Faslane on the Gare Loch and Firth of Clyde.

By the time the convoy of police cars and *Land Rover* had sped into Faslane, Lee had already managed to delay the scheduled memorial commemoration and instructed that, as a precautionary measure to ensure their safety, all dignitaries be placed in a secure unit under armed guard until her arrival to brief Naval Base Commander (Clyde), Commodore Donald McDougall about the reasons for taking such action. Instructions were given to a unit of the onsite Ministry Defence of Police to conduct an emergency yet discreet reconnaissance of the immediate vicinity with permission to arrest anyone without the required security clearance or whose behaviour gave rise to any hint of suspicion.

Gray led Sandy and Grace into a secure room and instructed a policeman to stand guard outside before joining Lee, who addressed the assembled dignitaries and explained that, given recent intelligence of a live and real terrorist threat, it was her recommendation that the parade should be cancelled with immediate effect.

'What intelligence precisely?' asked Robert Williams, the Secretary of State for Defence who was known for taking pride in his reputation as a stickler for detail and his penchant for hurtling straight to the nub of the matter regardless of whether he might ruffle a few feathers in the process. 'Do you have incontrovertible proof that such an attack is imminent?' Observing Lee's hesitation, the minister pounced with what he liked to think of as his characteristic forensic precision. 'Or is it your advice that we should cancel our plans at the faintest whiff of a terrorist threat based on nothing more than a hunch?'

'I don't have *incontrovertible* proof, but it *is* my belief that the threat is genuine – '

' – Then, in the absence of such proof, I should think that we continue as planned, mmm?' he mused, entirely oblivious to, so making no attempt to conceal, his condescension.

'With respect, minister, that's not for you to decide,' said Lee, disrespectfully. And deliberately so. 'I'll take my instructions from the Commodore.'

'Well Don,' said the minister, turning to the Commodore and, seemingly finding the turn of events a source of no small amusement, with a glint in his eye and a playful, self-satisfied smirk dimpling his cheeks, he teased, 'You know my position on the matter; what say you? Bearing in mind that, as we speak, we must surely be standing in the epicentre of one of the most secure and heavily guarded locations in the western hemisphere, no?', all but nudging the Commodore in the ribs and permitting himself a self-satisfied chuckle.

The Commodore nodded, seeing straight through the surface bonhomie to accept the unambiguous instruction he'd been given. 'The parade will proceed as planned upon the satisfactory conclusion of a brief – but thorough – reconnaissance of the immediate vicinity,' he said, addressing both the minister and Lee, who nodded her acknowledgement of his decision. She then made her excuses and vacated the room with Gray in tow.

~

'You asked me the other night about what I'd do in the event of a three-minute warning,' I mused, unable to resist the temptation to break the gnawing silence. 'And now I find myself at a nuclear base believed to be the target of an imminent terrorist attack. Is that coincidence?'

'What else could it be?'

Unable or unwilling to give voice to a festering alternative explanation, the dread of which I couldn't bring myself to confront, preferring instead to wrap myself in the relative safety of mystery, yet unable to prevent my thoughts from swirling around and around like dirty bathwater emptying down a gurgling plughole, I stretched for a branch to hang on to to save me from being dragged down by a powerful undertow, beating a hasty retreat from the precipice, battling against the dark undercurrent of my gathering suspicions.

Outside, a frustrated Lee, unprepared to hang around for the completion of the recce, instructed Gray to brief her about Faslane. As she knew he would, Gray had all the required facts and figures at his fingertips.

'Faslane's home to ten nuclear-powered submarines, but only four carry Trident nuclear missiles,' he began. 'Trident's an operational system of four Vanguard-class subs armed with Trident II D-5 ballistic missiles capable of delivering thermonuclear warheads. The Vanguard class comprises four boats: *Vanguard*, *Victorious*, *Vigilant* and *Vengeance* – each of which carries up to eight missiles and forty warheads. At least one of them is always on patrol to provide a continuous at-sea capability.'

'Find out which is currently at sea and – '

' – Where it is exactly,' anticipated Gray.

'Exactly.'

Moments later, Gray confirmed that *Vengeance* was currently operating at periscope depth in the Irish Sea, together with its exact coordinates, speed, and route.

'Are there any other vessels in the vicinity – civilian or military?' queried Lee.

Following a briefing with the Commodore's second-in-command, Gray was able to report back with the proximity of various fishing vessels and the evening crossing of the Stena Line *Superfast VII* roll-on/roll-off ferry operating between Belfast and Cairnryan.

'How many passengers does that ferry carry?'

Gray was now joined in person by the Commodore's second-in-command, who at first glance looked like a stereotypical talking uniform, straight-backed, waiting-for-orders-to-act-upon lapdog, who, without hesitation, answered matter-of-factly, '1,300 passengers. 660 cars.'

'Any news on the recce?' asked Lee.

'That's what I came to tell you,' said the lapdog. 'There's no sign of any suspicious activity. The parade's set to proceed as planned.'

'Thanks,' said Lee. 'We need to contact the ferry and *Vengeance* as a matter of urgency.'

'And tell them what exactly?'

'To be on red alert for a possible imminent terrorist attack.'

'Come with me,' instructed the lapdog, leading Lee and Gray through to the control room. En route they passed the dignitaries assembling for the commencement of the ceremonial parade.

'Something wrong?' asked Lee, impatiently, as soon as the smallest delay in receiving the reassurance she required made it evident to her that there was.

'I'm encountering some difficulty contacting *Vengeance*,' admitted the lapdog.

'Keep trying. How about the ferry?'

'Same story.'

'This is going down now,' said Lee. 'Get the Commodore.'

The rapidity of the resulting response ran up and down various chains of command with all the military precision and clockwork efficiency one might expect of a naval operation drilled to deal with such emergencies: perfectly machine-like, devoid of any time for doubt or room for consideration, drama or display of emotion. The second-in-command extricated the Commodore from the memorial ceremony who took the decision that he could not afford to wait until its completion before covering his arse by briefing the Secretary of State for Defence, whose first response was to cover his arse by briefing the Prime Minister whose first response was to cover his arse by convening an emergency Cobra meeting before passing the buck of responsibility back down to his Secretary of State for Defence who passed it back immediately to the Commodore. At no point did anyone offer an answer to Lee's question about what the estimated number of fatalities from a collision between a roll-on/roll-off ferry and a nuclear submarine armed with Trident nuclear missiles capable of delivering thermonuclear warheads would be. And at no point did anyone offer a challenge to her thesis that the communication failure affecting both vessels could be explained solely by a terrorist attack intent on creating such a cataclysmic collision.

A quick on-screen analysis of the routes of the two vessels revealed to the second-in-command that, given their current speed and direction, unless some kind of drastic intervention was set in motion, the vessels were set on a collision course calculated to occur half an hour hence. On receipt of this intelligence, adrenaline spiked, blood flow pumped faster, but still, logic retained control over emotion as the Commodore instructed a high-speed patrol boat containing a team of elite

SAS personnel with an estimated time of arrival of twenty minutes to race full throttle to *Vengeance* and do what needed to be done to prevent the collision. Simultaneously, a twin-engine helicopter carrying a parallel team of elite counter-terrorism SAS personnel on a parallel mission to the ferry was to be scrambled immediately. Lee demanded with a resolve that tolerated no objection that she would be on that helicopter. She was on that helicopter.

⌣

I wore a blank expression as I watched Grace consult her watch.

'I have a confession to make,' I announced. 'Contrary to what I suspected; I now know that Francisco's not Rose's father.'

'Oh? How come?'

'I subjected his DNA to a paternity test. So, I apologise for accusing you of sleeping with him.'

'Just because he's not Rose's father doesn't mean I didn't sleep with him.'

'True. Did you?'

'Yes. Many times. He's way better at it than you.'

'So, who is Rose's father?'

Grace rolled her eyes and, sighing like a recalcitrant teenager, checked her watch.

The 1,265 passengers aboard the roll-on/roll-off ferry sailing to Belfast were oblivious to the dramatic stand-off taking place on the bridge. The chief mate was holding a meat cleaver, freshly pinched from the galley kitchen, to the master's throat and threatening to hack off his head should the remaining bridge team dare take a step closer. The sightseers on the upper deck that had watched the helicopter approach were curious rather than concerned. It was not till the helicopter had lowered itself directly above them and hovered while the first of a team of black clad figures sporting balaclavas with assault rifles strapped to their backs had descended the rope to the deck and steadied it for the rest of the team to follow suit that curiosity was replaced by concern.

Simultaneously, while the crew members in the *Vengeance*'s sound room were aware of both the ferry and the approaching high speed patrol boat which they traced on sonar and radar and other sensors, they were unaware of the dramatic stand-off taking place in the Control Room where the nuclear engineer held a cleaver to the commanding officer's throat and threatened to hack off his head should the remaining Control Room team dare come a step closer.

But it was at this crucial juncture that the reactions to these meticulously pre-planned co-ordinated actions diverged to a markedly different degree, due to the manifest differences between a civilian and a military crew.

When the chief mate on the ferry held a cleaver to the master's throat and issued his threat should the bridge team dare come a step closer, the bridge team members stopped dead in their tracks for fear of their life and, unsure of what to do next, hesitated, awaiting further instruction. In contrast, when the nuclear engineer in the Control Room of the *Vengeance* deployed the same tactic, those members of Britain's Royal Marines from 43 Commando Fleet Protection present did not hesitate to act. Instead, they surged immediately, instinctively, primordially, as one brute unstoppable force, without thought for their own personal safety, and were upon the nuclear engineer in a violent frenzy of punching and kicking.

And though he flayed his cleaver desperately, the engineer's wrists were pinned and held and twisted and his blows rendered ineffectual so that although blood was spilt, the wounds inflicted were superficial rather than critical as the wannabe terroriser was overwhelmed in a collective act of impulsive bravery and any threat he had posed in a personal capacity extinguished. Though that was not to say that the threat of impending disaster as a consequence of an imminent catastrophic collision to which he had colluded in bringing to fruition had been averted.

With the clock continuing to tick down regardless, only minutes from a devastating crash, the second-in-command at Faslane was finally able to contact the master of *Vengeance* and alert him to the emergency at hand. The master wasted no time in instructing his helmsman to instruct that emergency diversionary action be taken, which involved decelerating, submerging and changing direction all at once. On the bridge of the ferry, the momentary stand-off between the chief mate holding a cleaver to the master's throat and the stalled bridge team was interrupted by the silent swift synchronised stealth surrounding from all angles of the SAS team.

Each team member had a C8 carbine assault rifle trained on the chief mate's temple. The same chief mate who, with evident mounting desperation, hesitated while insisting emphatically that on no account would he hesitate to kill the master. At this point, Lee, without losing eye contact with him, made a slow-motion show of placing her weapon on the floor, instructing her colleagues to follow suit. Speaking slowly, ever so slowly, and calmly and decisively and seemingly deaf to the chief mate's increasingly frantic exhortations that she stop, Lee sashayed straight up to him as if to whisper sweet nothings in his ear. In an instant, swift singular motion, she grabbed his wrist holding the cleaver and twisted herself into him before crouching and dragging him head over heels, topsy turvy spinning through the air, crashing flat on his back on the deck where, stunned, he found himself staring down the barrels of half a dozen assault rifles.

'Francisco García,' said Lee, brandishing the freshly secured meat cleaver 'Where is he?'

'I don't know,' blurted the captive. 'Honestly.'

'Honestly?' mimicked Lee. 'Well, if we're being *honest*, I have my doubts about your *honesty*. Experience tells me that only torture or an act of extreme violence which will require emergency surgery to prevent death will yield *honesty*. And since time's of the essence, I don't have the luxury of indulging in torture.'

Then, to her SAS colleagues, she instructed, 'Hold him down. Steady.' The team duly pinned the captive's spread-eagled arms and legs to the floor as Lee grabbed a handful of his hair in her left hand and, in her right, brought down the cleaver, removing the hair from his crown, together with a sizeable chunk of his scalp. The chief mate howled as the blow brought forth a sizeable puddle of maroon to well then geyser from atop his head and run crimson rivulets down his temples.

'It's only a suggestion, but there's a couple of factors you might wish to consider,' posited Lee. 'Firstly, the next blow from this cleaver will hack your head off, just as you'd threatened to do to the master here. Secondly, we already have your colleague on Vengeance at hand, so that if you choose not to corroborate, we'll simply... *encourage* him to do so in your stead. Finally… d'you really think that, given the luxury of choice, Francisco would opt to lose *his* head for you rather than live to fight another day?'

~⌒~

I wore a blank expression as I watched Grace check her watch.

'I guess I just don't get you,' I said.

'And you never will.'

'Why? 'Cos I'm so shallow?'

''Cos you're so full of light,' she corrected, checking her watch for the umpteenth time. 'It pours out of you. You don't have a shadow to lurk in. And there's nothing you can do about it.'

'Why do you keep checking your watch?' I asked. It was not till I'd given voice to the question that I was gripped by a horror at the possibility of her answer. 'Tell me you're not part of this.'

'I'm not part of this,' she said, checking her watch.

twenty-one

fall
from
grace

'The sub plot was real enough – but it was also a subterfuge – '

' – how so?' interrupted Gray.

'If successful, the devastation caused would've been colossal and dragged our entire focus west, leaving the capital exposed and vulnerable,' explained Lee. 'Get yourself over to Edinburgh. At most we've an hour or so to prevent a devastating terrorist attack, though, beyond confirmation that the target's Edinburgh Castle and that a large-scale bomb's involved, we don't as yet know what to expect. It seems our captive informant was sealed in a blissful bubble of ignorance. Take Young and Robertson with you – and keep a close eye on them. I don't know what it is exactly, whether they're innocent... or ignorant yet implicated... or complicit... I can't quite put my finger on it... yet. But I do know I'm unconvinced by their innocent little *Babes in the Wood*, *Hansel and Gretel* routine. Something's niggling me. I've a nagging suspicion that they might yet have a bearing on how all this pans out.'

'Understood. And what about you?'

'We're taking the helicopter!' shouted Lee, straining to be heard over the rapidly approaching whirr of rotor blades overhead. 'All going well, we should get there well before you!'

The tension was palpable as the live feed of the roar of a Spitfire taking off from Edinburgh Airport shook the air, signalling the opening fanfare as the Massed Pipes and Drums marched through the castle gatehouse into the centre of the esplanade to the rousing pipe band, just as they had done on each night of the last three weeks. The apprehension mounted with the introduction and exit of each new performer throughout the duration of the spectacle until, as a rousing finale, the ensemble assembled for a traditional ceilidh before retreating as a Lone Piper appeared high on the castle ramparts. The pregnant pause at the conclusion of his lament was shattered only by an eruption of fireworks. A Spitfire swooping overhead sparked a rousing chorus from spectators of *Auld Lang Syne*.

The reconvened convoy's return journey east along the M8 might have felt long-drawn-out to me, speed slowed by *déjà vu* and wheels seemingly congealed in thick treacle gloop, such was the toxic mingling of the festering silence between myself and Grace with Gray's blatant distrust. In reality it was completed at a speed comfortably in excess of 100mph from one end of the motorway to the other. It concluded at the top of the Royal Mile where we disembarked and were ushered brusquely through heavily guarded police barriers for a debriefing by Lee in the command centre. This was located at a vantage point on the castle ramparts overseeing the esplanade where numerous screens and monitors scanned the crowd as police and security personnel were instructed to be on alert for any signs of disturbance.

'If either of you two have anything useful to contribute; now's the time,' said Lee, noticing me fire a furtive glance in Grace's direction.

'Is there something you wish to share?' she probed, adopting the tone of a reassuring schoolteacher attempting to coax a contribution from the awkward kid at the back of the class forever attempting to hide behind a classmate. 'Anything that might help prevent the mass casualties resulting from a major terrorist incident?'

'Nothing,' I said, averting my eyes and hanging my head, as if adopting obediently the very persona Lee's tone had attributed to me.

Lee looked over to Gray, who took his unspoken cue.

'You look as if you could do with a brew,' he addressed Grace. 'Let's see if we can go find ourselves a cuppa.' He led her off to a makeshift canteen.

'What is it you wanted to tell me?' asked Lee, picking up her interrogation from where she'd left off, adopting an even softer, more intimate tone, with a shift to a lower timbre accompanied by a slight tilt of the head that did not go unnoticed. 'Sandy, it's now or never,' she insisted. 'There's something you want to tell me, but you felt uneasy raising in Grace's presence,' she probed gingerly, as if fighting to resist the temptation to reach over, gently touch the back of my hand and give it a reassuring squeeze.

'It's nothing really, but…'

'But?'

'Well…' I sighed. 'I'm sure it's nothing …'

'But?'

'But… I'm starting to have some doubts…'

'About?'

'About my faith… in Grace.'

'And why's that?'

'Because… because hurt people hurt people.'

⌒

Then it was Grace's turn to find herself alone in the command centre with Lee, Gray having read the situation and initiated a return trip to the canteen with myself in tow this time round.

'D'you have something you want to tell me?' asked Lee, in a tone more abrupt than that deployed for myself, in the manner of a harassed teacher at the end of her tether acutely conscious of the ticking clock, intent only on establishing the facts of an alleged transgression to her satisfaction as efficiently and as practicably as possible in order to ascertain how best to proceed and what retribution, if any, was warranted as soon as she was able.

'About what?'

'About Francisco.'

'?'

'Sandy thought you might have something you wanted to… confess.'

Grace contorted her face into a portrait of contemptuous derision.

'He's worried about you,' said Lee. 'And he blames himself for not… '

'For not *what*?'

'For not being there for you when you needed him most, when you needed help. As he tells it, it sounds to me like you've been struggling to cope; that you've suffered, *are* suffering, from a desperate sense of hopelessness… something about which I might have some… insight.'

'Well, he *wasn't there* when I needed him, so maybe he's right to blame himself – '

' – but *you* don't blame him, do you? You blame yourself.'

It was a comment, an accusation even, that piqued Grace's interest; the possibility that this woman she barely knew might have some inkling of her muted, deep-rooted resentment. And before she knew what she was doing, Grace found herself opening up and speaking voluntarily of her fall from grace. She spoke of the sense of suffocating under the intensity of the pressure to experience, the expectation to *feel* unbridled elation, the admittance of its absence, the impossibility of conceiving a time when it would be possible to accept that absence, the hollow lonely bottomless well into which she fell, tumbling into a loss of feeling, an interminable loss of feeling till nothing mattered anymore and she was left without sensation at her core. Senseless. Rendered void.

'Whatever the feeling... or lack of feeling... I don't seem to be able to... describe it without resorting to metaphor,' she reflected.

'That's what metaphors are for: to help us try to describe the indescribable,' counselled Lee.

'It was as if, by giving birth, I died. Or at least part of me. Some essential part of me that made me *me*. And I resented her for that. For condemning me to an infinite burden of responsibility and for... amputating some intrinsic part of my identity. And for demanding I sacrifice my freedom to be shackled to the development of her identity. And I was plagued by the mystery at the heart of her identity. And what that mystery might mean. And I kept my toxic misgivings to myself and that riddled me with poison from the inside out to the point where nothing mattered any more. I resented *them* for planting that toxic seed of doubt. And I resented her... Rose, all the while knowing, that she was entirely innocent and undeserving of any such bitterness. And I'm ashamed, so utterly *ashamed*, at my embittering resentment. But incapable to do anything about it. Which only compounds my crushing sense of shame.'

'And where does Francisco García come into this?' pressed Lee, acutely conscious that time was of the essence. Grace sighed, wiped her eyes, sniffed, and answered with a question.

'Are you familiar with Dalí's paranoiac-critical method?

'Why?'

'Well, back when we first met Francisco in Costa Brava, he introduced me to some of Dalí's double images – *Slave Market with the Disappearing Bust of Voltaire, Swans Reflecting Elephants, Metamorphosis of Narcissus* – and I had a kind of... *Gestalt switch*. A change of perspective that taught me to doubt my perception of reality; that *reality* might be nothing other than an illusion. And then he introduced me to this...' She unstrapped her watch and showed Lee a small tattoo that had been hidden underneath the worn brown leather strap on the inside of her wrist:

侘寂

'Wabi-sabi,' said Lee.

'An appreciation of the beauty of imperfection; of *transience*,' nodded Grace, fastening her watchstrap. 'And the combination of these concepts, these *aesthetics*, jolted me. I felt... *enlightened* by a paradigm shift from the micro to the macro and found that I'd become almost impervious to the concerns of the individual. Everything's illusion. *Nothing*'s real. Nothing matters. Everything's fluid. Everything's nothing. Francisco helped me... understand that it's only by experiencing tragedy that the curtain of fantasy can be raised to... expose the true nature of reality in all its glorious naked horror. And he helped me realise that it was my... duty to try to raise that curtain and expose the sham that the walking dead take to be reality for the artificiality it is. For the sake of humanity.'

An interminable silence that lasted only a moment or two was broken, eventually, by a slow handclap.

'Bravo,' said Anderson, making his presence felt from the margins. 'That was quite a performance. But I'm not buying it. I think you're telling us what you think we want to hear. Are you really trying to tell me that, as a result of suffering some kind of post-partum depression, coupled with some oversimplistic misinterpretation of some Dalí paintings and some wabi-sabi mumbo jumbo thrown in for good measure, you were somehow groomed by Francisco into playing a part in his terrorist plot? Well, I, for one, remain unconvinced.'

Grace smiled slyly, raised her hands in surrender and shook her head in mock disbelief.

'Where does Sandy fit in to all this?' asked Lee, noticing myself and Gray eavesdropping from the doorway.

'Sandy's as innocent and ignorant as Rose,' said Grace, dismissively. 'He knows nothing.'

And then, stepping from the shadows, an unfamiliar, tentative voice said, 'I don't think you're Francisco's hand puppet. I think you're the puppet master.'

An awkward pause stalled proceedings momentarily as the gathering turned its surprised attention towards determining the identity of the interloper and to hear what possible justification he might have for his impertinent intervention at such a critical juncture, with the exception of Anderson, whose back straightened instinctively with satisfaction on recognising the accusation as having emanated from the lips of his timorous colleague. DC Whittaker had, finally, found his voice.

'After all,' continued Whittaker, looking at Grace directly. 'You're right here right now while your stooge's intent on committing the ultimate sacrifice. You say that Dalí taught you to *doubt your perception of reality*, but you and I both know that Dalí's just the joker in the pack of surrealists whose king was André Breton. It was Breton, was it not, who said that '*the simplest surrealist act is walking into a crowd with a loaded gun and firing at random*'? We forget at our peril that the surrealists were originally a revolutionary movement. Maybe your *mission*, and that of your Amino acolytes, is nothing less than the resurrection of surrealism by a meticulously planned terrorist atrocity exhibition. An *homage* to the anarchic spirit of surrealism as a *spectacular* phantasmagorical transgressive act of apolitical shock theatre of the absurd.'

And then, glimpsing Grace steal an instinctive glance at the Spitfire's soars and swoops and loop-de-loops, something in her expression... something lacking ... a certain lack of grace, in a eureka moment of inspired intuition Lee knew, even if she could not explain exactly how she knew, that the Spitfire was packed with explosives and piloted by García intent on executing a kamikaze nosedive into the castle ramparts above the esplanade and sending the shattered remnants of the castle to crash down on the mass of helpless spectators below in a spectacle of horror and devastation.

twenty-two

coup
de
grâce

'García's piloting that Spitfire,' Lee informed Gray. 'I need to speak to him. Now.'

Gray made it happen while simultaneously scrambling the SWAT team and instructing its members to assume position and train their sites on the Spitfire while awaiting Lee's command to fire.

This was the coup de grâce Francisco had dedicated these last years orchestrating. The fulfilment of his visionary destiny as the redeemer, the messiah of truth, the destroyer of fake. The resurrector of beauty through artifice, through doubt, through terror. The culmination of years of manipulation aided and abetted by a determined dabbling in double-dealing, procurement of a convincing, if entirely fabricated, ID as a fully qualified pilot (papered over by an intense training programme at a clandestine airstrip in Libya) and help from various friends, erstwhile lovers, traitors, spooks and mercenaries. Francisco had managed eventually to wheedle for himself the position of co-pilot in the Spitfire, a position he assumed with a suicide belt packed with ball bearings, nails, screws and bolts and armed with a detonator, strapped to his chest and a syringe at hand with which to anesthetise the pilot by jagging a jugular vein from behind as soon as they were airborne.

Lee donned a headset, introduced herself, and set the scene.

'Francisco García, I need you to listen to me,' she began. 'Two *Eurofighter Typhoons* armed with Meteor active radar guided air-to-air missiles have been scrambled from RAF Lossiemouth and are locked onto your coordinates ready to shoot you down as soon as I give the command – '

' – give the command,' interrupted Francisco's disembodied electrolarynx voice. 'This is a suicide mission. Your threat's meaningless.'

'Your mission's meaningless. The indiscriminate slaughter of hundreds of innocent people! To what end?'

'It's an end in itself.'

Frustrated at the futility of seeking to reason with a devotee of a nihilistic cult of the absurd, Lee tore off the headset. After an eternal moment of torment, in a last-ditch effort at conjuring a death-defying miraculous intervention to realise a shift in perspective like Dalí turning elephants into swans, she offered it to Grace. Grace looked at Lee impassively, as if from behind a dense curtain of fog drawn over a vale of tears.

In desperation, I rushed forward to plead my case.

'Grace,' I begged, taking her cold hands in mine. 'I don't believe *any* of this. If you've had anything to do with this then I've never known you and nothing makes sense…'

'You've never known me,' she said. 'Nothing makes sense.'

I searched her face for enlightenment. It was blank. Expressionless. Featureless. Then, as if emerging from a trance, Grace grabbed the headset from Lee, placed it over her ears and, looking me in the eye, in a voice calm with decision said, 'Time for an immediate communion with the whole, absolute vision through the grace of truth, by divine grace. Set the controls for the heart of the sun.'

'Scream thy last scream,' answered Francisco, observing that he had just then become the filling in a *Eurofighter*

Typhoon sandwich. He swooped and dived into a couple of barrel rolls above and below the rust-coloured cantilevers of the Forth Rail Bridge. He executed a victory roll up and under the Forth Road Bridge, unable to shake off his twin pursuers. He corkscrewed towards the castle esplanade, spiralling straight for Grace, who watched transfixed, mesmerised, paralysed, engulfed by his trajectory as, salivating at the prospect of annihilation, giddy at the imminence of self-destruction, Francisco did not deviate from his date with destiny. Anderson and Whittaker leapt into action, rushing to drag myself and Grace from harm's way. While I capitulated, Grace turned herself into an immovable object to meet the unstoppable force, leaving the policemen no option but to abandon her to surrender herself to her fate. The taut, twitchy-fingered SWAT team's patience was at the end of its tether, all set to explode as Lee delayed further the command to fire till the last possible moment when the twin *Eurofighter Typhoons* tore off and spun and soared upwards suddenly in precise symmetrical sonic boom jet streams as the Spitfire careened straight ahead.

'Fire,' she said. The SWAT team ejaculated a furious, if ineffectual, fusillade. Lee removed her Glock 17 from its holster, glanced at Gray and said, 'Time to get real,' firing a round straight into the Spitfire's tail plane. The Spitfire spat fire and juddered violently. Francisco, in the same nano-second, lost the fight to regain control. At the last possible point, instead of exploding head on into Grace and obliterating everyone in the immediate vicinity in a Dalí-inspired inferno of heaven or hell, the Spitfire's undercarriage grazed the castle ramparts and careened off wildly corkscrewing like a fizzing firework, arcing upwards over the esplanade then nosediving into Arthur's Seat to erupt in a fantastical inferno at the apex of the long extinct volcano. Though undeniably spectacular, the craved devastation from the explosion was nullified by its location on the dark deserted hillside a safe distance from the castle's bustling ramparts.

afterword

my mum can stop time (the disintegration of the persistence of memory)

Noticing that it was my mum calling, I hesitated until Kerr answered his phone before deciding to answer mine. Just as I was set to launch into my well-worn admonition for her having interrupted me at work, my mum stopped time with a two-word announcement.

'There's been a development,' said Kerr, slamming down his newspaper print-stained receiver. 'The police are waiting for you in reception.' Then, noticing my stricken expression. 'You OK?'

'I'll call you right back,' I told mum, nodding to Kerr.

I met agents Lee and Gray and DS Anderson in reception and, immediately conscious of the oppressive tension, ushered them straight into the conference room without delay.

'Grace escaped,' said Lee, skipping the social niceties altogether, before we were even seated. 'It seems that DC Whittaker, Anderson's colleague, was not all that he seemed.'

'What happened?' I asked.

An ashamed Anderson sighed heavily. Then, with infinite reluctance, but as concisely as he was able, related how, on the basis of her own confession the previous evening, Whittaker and himself had arrested Grace Robertson at The Tattoo on suspicion of having plotted to commit a terrorist act, read her her rights and duly handcuffed her and bundled her into a waiting police car led by two police motorcycles for interrogation at nearby St. Leonard's Police Station. But before they arrived at their destination, they were diverted up a side street by what he now knew to be bogus road repair paraphernalia, signs and workmen, where they were duly ambushed by a balaclava-wearing, machine gun-toting gang who swiftly deployed their machine guns to despatch any threat posed by the police motorcyclists before demanding, at gunpoint, that the occupants of the vehicle vacate it immediately. At this point Anderson was pistol-whipped, lost consciousness temporarily and slumped to the ground, coming to a short interval later to find himself abandoned and handcuffed to a bicycle rack at the side of the cobbled lane with blood seeping from a gash on his temple.

'Grace took Whittaker hostage?' I asked.

'No,' sighed Anderson.

'Why are you so sure?'

'Because it was Whittaker who knocked me out.'

'Whittaker was an inside man?'

Struggling to muster the effort required to voice a confirmation, Anderson contented himself with the slightest of nods as an inadequate substitute.

'There's more you should know,' said Lee, launching into her own summary of recent events.

'Within half an hour of the plane crash, search and rescue teams were combing Arthur's Seat with instructions to pinpoint the site of impact, examine the wreckage and rescue any survivors. At 23:00Hrs they located the smoking wreckage and a hazmat suited and booted team of crime scene examiners from the Scottish Police Authority's forensics services team was summoned to preserve, examine, and record evidence. And remove a badly charred body from the pilot's seat.

'The remains, presumed to be those of Francisco García,

were sent to the morgue for an emergency post-mortem. I received the results an hour ago. They confirm that the corpse was *not* Francisco García, but, DNA analysis revealed, one Captain Jim Mackenzie – the pilot of the Spitfire whom, it seems, had been injected with an anaesthetic prior to the crash, presumably by García, the co-pilot. Further, an extensive examination of unseen footage taken by BBC camera crews at the Tattoo was able to pick up a blurred image. Once processed through enhanced imaging technology, this revealed that a camouflaged khaki-coloured parachute had been deployed just prior to the Spitfire crashing into Arthur's Seat in a ball of flame to drift gently down on the far side of the hill into the heart of darkness. Entirely unnoticed.'

'Are you telling me that Francisco, together with Whittaker and Grace, have all absconded?' I asked.

'An extensive manhunt has been set in motion,' said Lee. 'We received various unconfirmed reports of activity at Leith Docks during the night, with a sighting by a fishing vessel of an unfamiliar speed boat heading out to sea.'

'So, they could be anywhere by now?'

'Which brings me to the purpose of our visit,' said Lee. 'Sandy, I need you to think very carefully. Is there anything, *anything* you can think of that might help us narrow our search and help us find Grace?'

'If there's one thing I know I know, it's that I never knew, and never will, know Grace,' I said.

I then decided to share with the room the contents of the two-word phone call my mum had made an eternity of moments earlier.

'Rose's missing,' I said. 'My daughter. She's been abducted. From my mum's house. In Motherwell. If I were seeking Grace, and I am, if only to find Rose, I'd start my search there.'

postscript

a return to the dalí triangle

No sooner had the paper run *Fake Flowers*, my definitive account of the events leading up to Rose's abduction, than it was denounced by a rampant army of anonymous social media keyboard warrior conspiracy theorists and armchair detectives. One of the most memorable attacks accused it as '*fake. Nothing other than a desperate plea for attention. A self-justificatory fabricated work of fiction. A blatantly cynical attempt to hijack the misery lit gravy train by a sad self-seeking fame-hungry wannabe auto biographer determined to cash in on casting himself as the 'woe is me' innocent victim crying out at the injustices of the world for a pity party.*'

It was when I was tasked by Kerr to pen a piece to rebut the conspiracy theorists, robustly reaffirm the veracity of my account and expose their far-fetched fantasies for the unfounded caprices that they are that I realised I was disembodied and living in an incorporeal surreal universe where each passing day was marked by my memories slipping like a clockface melting in the heat of the sun from the firm grip of reality into the realms of the surreal. I found, to my dismay, that I was lost in a featureless landscape of self-doubt. No longer convinced of my ability to distinguish fact from fiction.

Finding myself incapable of writing the piece he'd requested, rather than penning my self-defence and professing my truthfulness and innocence unequivocally, I opted instead to inform Kerr of my impromptu decision to hand in my notice. This was a course of action which served only to confirm my guilt in the eyes of the conspiracy theorists. And I *did* feel guilty. Even if I couldn't explain why. To myself or anyone else. All I knew was that my quest, the only way to rid myself of that corroding sense of culpability, was to find Rose safe and unharmed.

Having lost what little faith I had to start with in the authorities' ability to find my daughter, I decided to take matters into my own hand. The consensus of informed opinion seemed to be that Francisco, Grace and Rose, together with the rest of The Amino, had managed to flee the country, either together or separately, and find their way back to Spain under fake IDs. I set about determining how I might relocate there for as long as it took to find Rose. And so it was that, with a little help from a friend of a friend, I managed to land a position teaching English as a foreign language at a school in Girona. My new employer helped me find a nearby one bedroom apartment to rent in Call, the city's Jewish Quarter.

Whenever not teaching classes or losing whole evenings staring at my laptop searching arbitrarily for clues online, I took to prowling Call's labyrinth of medieval alleyways and cobbled streets in a haphazard manhunt. And each weekend I'd hop on my *Moped* to explore Costa Brava's rugged coastline, from Portbou down to Blanes, from every possible angle. Within and without the Dalí Triangle.

 ⌒

Around a year later, as a brief intermission in search of some temporary respite from my usual fruitless and frustrating morning hunt, in preparation for that afternoon's planned exploration of L'Estartit, I found myself sunbathing on the beach nursing a familiar sense of *déjà vu* garnished with a persistent infatuated longing for *la vie en rose*. I sought to rid myself of my slough of despond with a cleansing dip in the Med where I could recalibrate my thoughts to the rhythm of my breath resounding through my snorkel.

Pacified by a gently bobbing buoyancy, balmed by sunrays

and sea, I resurfaced to clear my mask of mist. Treading water, I stole a glance back to shore. Through my salt water blurred vision, I glimpsed an apparition. A man and a woman with a young girl heading from the beach. Something about their familiarity as a cohesive family unit stabbed my temporary sense of calm through the heart, leaving me floundering in the sea like a freshly hooked fish fighting for survival. Having swum ashore as fast as I was able, I combed the beach to no avail, circling back to retrieve my clothes to embark on my planned investigation of the town's bustling shops and cafes.

When I spied a small rose gold fake flower resting in the head-shaped indentation of my striped beach towel I felt myself dissolving from reality into a surreal Dalí landscape.

CONTEMPORARY SCOTTISH FICTION
FROM RYMOUR BOOKS

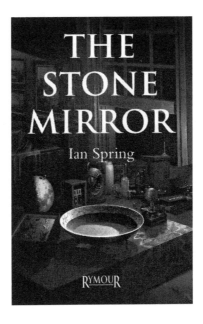

A COLLECTION of short fictions, mostly about death,
in which a man turns into a house (or vice versa),
angels appear on the earth (but far too often).
Doctor Faust in undeniably damned (several times),
decapitation (and cardiectomy) fail to prove fatal and
various other literary ploys occur (or fail to occur).